THE DEMIGOD
Complex

BRIMSTONE  INC.

THE
DEMIGOD
Complex

BRIMSTONE ✪ INC.

ABIGAIL OWEN

Entangled Publishing, LLC
10940 S Parker Rd
Suite 327
Parker, CO 80134
rights@entangledpublishing.com

Amara is an imprint of Entangled Publishing, LLC.

Edited by Heather Howland
Cover design by Bree Archer
Cover photography by LightField Studios/Shutterstock
wacomka and DenisTangneyJr/GettyImages

Manufactured in the United States of America

First Edition February 2020

To Jill—my sister of the heart. No matter how long we're apart, we pick right up where we left off—only older, wiser, and with more kids. Love you!

Chapter One

Lyleia Naiad stared at the white envelope sitting on her desk, trying to pluck up the courage to march into her boss's office and hand it to him.

Suck it up, and just do it.

Just resign. Give her two weeks' notice and walk away. Not as easy as it sounded. She'd been trying for two weeks to pluck up the courage. The trouble was she didn't really want to leave. She loved her job. It had given her life a sense of purpose.

But she had to disappear again. She should have known coming out of hiding, even just into the shadows at the edges, was a bad idea.

She had no proof, but last night was the second time in a month that she suspected someone had been in her apartment. Running anytime that instinct kicked in had kept her alive for centuries.

Which meant she had to go. Soon.

"Hey." Mike Morgan, the lead lawyer for Dioskouri Enterprises, walked into her office.

In the same instant, the intercom on her desk came to life with Castor Dioskouri's voice.

"Lyleia."

A barked order she had no problem interpreting as "get your ass in here."

Lyleia, who went by Leia to everyone but her boss, winced. Holding up a finger to the man standing on the other side of her desk, she pressed the intercom button. "I have Mike Morgan with me. Two minutes?"

Silence.

She gave Castor another few seconds, then, assuming he was okay with waiting, lifted her gaze to the head lawyer of Dioskouri Enterprises. She held out her hand to accept the paperwork he'd brought. "Thanks, Mike. I'll get his signature and have this back to you by end of day."

She stood and smoothed down her gray pencil skirt and white, button-down blouse and patted her hair into place. Then she disconnected her computer from the docking station.

But Mike didn't leave. Instead, he casually hitched a hip on her desktop, pushing papers around. Leia held in a sigh as her fingers itched to fix the small upset to her perfectly ordered work area.

"When are you going to go out with me?" Mike asked with what she was sure most women found to be a charming smile. The lawyer, while excellent at his job, was a player with a capital *P*. Not her style at all. It took a lot more than charm and looks to impress a nymph. Even an ex-water nymph who'd failed to protect her spring.

"Never. When are you going to stop asking?" She gave Mike a gentle push to get off her desk and came around the side to head into Castor's office.

Mike got up but didn't make a move to leave. "Just one little date?"

She shook her head, amused despite herself, and pointed at the door. "You're a great coworker, but that's all it will ever be. Now shoo."

"Friday?"

Leia crossed her arms, getting annoyed.

"Mike. Did you need something?"

The dark rumble of Castor's voice sounded behind her, even more irritated than over the intercom. Leia spun on her heel to find him standing in the doorway, glowering like a bear with a thorn in its paw.

"I was dropping off the Metro paperwork for your signature." Mike strolled to the door. "See you later, Leia."

She nodded but otherwise didn't pay attention to his departure. Her entire focus was on the man standing in front of her. Tall, dark, and handsome was a cliché that didn't begin to cover the pure energy and power radiating from his lean form.

As had happened from her first day working for him, Castor's presence pulled a visceral response from her. *Why the hell can't I turn off my body around him?*

Damn the gods who'd ruined her life. She had despised them, werewolves, and anything to do with gods or their demigod offspring.

Until this one.

Somehow, Castor had snuck under all her defenses.

Not that she'd ever act on her feelings, especially not now. But even if she wasn't about to disappear again, she couldn't. The man still grieved his wife. He didn't speak of her ever, but Leia had heard the rumors. He'd lost her not long into their marriage, which had to be hard…knowing he'd go through an immortal life without his love.

Castor wanted nothing to do with relationships.

How had all those other assistants before her not caught the "loner" vibes the man threw out? No wonder he'd hired

Brimstone, Inc., to send him someone like her.

All the more reason to get herself under control.

Just as she had every other day, Leia ruthlessly squashed her feelings, the same way she'd grind a cockroach under her stiletto heel. Even when they were for a six-foot-three, Armani-suit-wearing chiseled tower of temptation with blue eyes and a heart big enough to rescue the world, though he liked to hide it behind a scowl.

Like now. His eyes practically shot bolts of lightning as he glared at Mike's departing back.

She stepped forward, assuming he'd move out of the way to usher her into his office. Only he didn't, his glower softening as he turned his gaze on her.

Only now she was very much in his space, inhaling the spice of his aftershave and the fresh-air scent of his skin. The heat radiating from him penetrated both his suit and her clothes. Demigods ran hot—something about all that supernatural power coursing through their veins. When she was a young water nymph, she'd imagined it would be nice to snuggle up to one in a pond, like her own walking hot springs generator.

But that had been before she'd lost her spring.

Instead of getting out of her way, Castor leaned forward, crowding her more. "Does Mike bother you often?"

"Did you know Marsha in acquisitions is pregnant? I assume you'll want to arrange a shower?"

"That's not what I asked."

Distracting him with other topics sometimes worked. Not this time, apparently. She raised her eyebrows coolly. "*Mike* doesn't bother me at all." As opposed to the man blocking her way. She was proud her words hadn't come out all husky and needy sounding. In control, even if she wasn't really.

"So, you wanted him to ask you out?" Doubt colored the words.

She stared at his top button, which was undone, as was his tie, exposing the kissable hollow at the base of his neck. Dang. Now she was wondering what licking that spot might taste like.

No, she wasn't, because she didn't let herself think things like that about her boss. Her *demigod* boss. Her *billionaire* demigod boss who had more money than Midas, more power than he knew what to do with, and whose only requirement for his assistant was that they not bother him with things like unwanted, unreciprocated feelings.

A wish she deeply understood.

Why were they having this conversation again? "I can handle Mike."

He reached out and tipped her chin up, forcing her to meet his gaze. "So, he needs handling?"

Her skin tingled at his touch. That happened every time he touched her. *Because he's the son of Zeus...and lightning,* she ruthlessly reminded herself.

Time to put a stop to this or next she'd be throwing herself into his arms. She rolled her eyes. "You can put away your cape, Superman. I don't need saving today."

His jaw tensed, mouth pinching. She recognized that stubborn look. Castor wasn't going to give this up. The man had a god complex a mile wide—a need to rescue anything he deemed helpless. In the old days, demigods spent most of their time fighting monsters or rescuing princesses or towns. He seemed to have found other ways to channel that drive.

Not for her, though. No thanks.

What she needed was a diversion. "I need to talk to you about something."

He dropped his hand and stepped back. "What?"

Granted, distracting him with her resignation might not be the smartest of moves. Even if all that intensity had shifted away from the topic of Mike. Still, this had to be done.

"Let's sit down first," she said.

Castor frowned, then finally moved out of the way. Oxygen returned to her lungs as he led her inside his office. The view of the Austin skyline from his office never got old. She would miss this city more than most.

But it would be Castor she missed most of all.

. . .

Castor sat in a fancy chrome chair behind a modern glass desk and leaned back, the supple leather not even creaking, as he directed his gaze to the woman across the way.

Even this far away from her, Leia's rainy-day scent, the hallmark of a water nymph, drifted around him. Drawing him in.

He would always associate water with her now. These days the sound of rain, or the flash of sunlight on a lake as he flew his plane overhead, or, hell, even the sound of his shower put him in mind of her. And left him hard and aching every fucking morning.

Damn and blast.

One simple request had led to this.

When he had hired Brimstone, Inc., to find him a new executive assistant, he'd asked the owner/operator, Delilah, for one thing. Someone who wouldn't ever fall in love—or lust—with him. Something that was damn near impossible for humans and supernaturals alike. Most couldn't resist the ancient god's blood coursing through his veins.

Delilah had managed to provide the perfect solution to his dilemma…a nymph. How had he not thought of that himself? After all, he knew the stories…

The gods had "blessed" nymphs to give and receive extraordinary pleasure. Essentially, making the guardians of nature—minor deities in their own right—into the gods' own personal sex toys. To retaliate, the goddesses, sick of all the bastard children the randy gods kept churning out, had given nymphs a doozy of a gift—the ability to resist any sexual temptation.

Hera, Zeus's wife herself, and goddess of marriage and birth, was known to have been jealous and resentful of all her husband's illegitimate offspring. Castor should know, since he was one. The goddess couldn't stand him and his brother Pollux. No doubt she'd been the one to come up with the idea of the counter blessing. Not so much to help nymphs as to screw the gods, her husband in particular.

Regardless of the hows and whys, Leia could resist his raw, innate sexuality. She could, with ease, ignore the vibes Castor couldn't help but put out.

More than that, his EA had *Not Interested*—or, more accurately, he suspected, *The Gods Suck*—tattooed across her forehead.

Something to do with how she lost her spring. He didn't have all the details, but whatever happened wasn't pretty. Now she hated the gods, and by association, their demigod children.

But what he hadn't counted on was how *he* would react to Leia.

Respecting her past, and his own edict, he'd kept his distance, kept things in the strictly professional box. But no one else talked back to him like she did. Or got his blood pumping like she did. Or challenged him to be better, think smarter, like she did.

He had a sinking feeling that he was falling ass over head in love with her. What the fuck was he supposed to do about that?

Especially when the woman had been trying to resign for a month and he was running out of ways to stave off the inevitable.

She had no idea he knew, either. As she'd left his office one evening, a white envelope had fluttered to the floor. Castor had moved around his desk to pick it up and had his hand outstretched for the doorknob to take it into Leia's adjoining office only to pause at the sight of his name printed in her neat, looping handwriting.

Curious, he'd pulled out the single, typewritten page.

Dear Mr. Dioskouri…

Not since the first week, when he'd corrected her a thousand times, had Leia addressed him so formally.

Then he'd kept reading. *I hereby tender my resignation…*

After reeling in shock, the thought of losing her hit him with the force of a lightning strike, the emotion so visceral his lungs had hurt with each indrawn breath. A sensation he hadn't appreciated, given that he'd been walking this earth with as few emotions as possible since losing his wife. That was the moment he'd realized that liking, respect, and a physical attraction that simmered through him at the oddest moments weren't fleeting, but falling for her hard.

Almost as much of a shock as her letter.

He'd tucked the damn thing into a pile of papers on her desk after she'd left for the day and said nothing.

That had been a month ago, and he'd been scrambling ever since to figure out why in Hades she wanted to leave and what he could do to make her stay.

Fuck all apparently. Because the woman looked resolved to resign right here, right now.

Leia took her usual leather armchair across the way.

Then she seemed to register his expression and blinked.

There. Satisfaction sparked inside him, electricity sizzling down nerve endings. A flash of something lit her eyes that was beyond professional. Something that heated his blood. She wasn't disinterested.

At least, he didn't think she wasn't. She was so damn

hard to read.

The flash was there, then gone in another blink and she raised her eyebrows, giving him that look. The one that said she thought maybe he needed to lie down for a minute.

"What's the latest on the Morning Star project?" he asked, deliberately trying to make it harder for her to jump into resigning.

"I..." She hesitated, glanced at something in her pile of papers. No doubt that damn envelope.

"I assume you've heard from Lance?" he prompted. He could be ruthless when he had to.

Only another beat of hesitation, then she nodded. "He has sent in a new report on the progress. He's asking for another six months."

"He can have three," he said.

She nodded and noted the task.

Castor sat back and fiddled with a pen. "Actually, scratch that. I'll take care of it and talk to him directly."

Not even a blink or hesitation. She merely nodded again and adjusted her notes, then glanced up. "Anything else?"

A loaded question if he'd ever heard one.

"I need you to accompany me on a trip."

Chapter Two

Leia blinked. What the hell just happened? She'd had the perfect opportunity to hand him her resignation letter and she'd chickened out. Like a cowardly hen who clucked all the way into her coop to hide.

She should speak up. Right now.

She opened her mouth to do just that—

"Tell me about the trip," is what came out instead. "Where will we be going?"

"Colorado. Rocky Mountain National Park. Specifically, we'll be staying outside the park at the Stanley Hotel."

She'd made a note to check the map for the closest city to fly into, probably Denver, though a private airstrip might be closer. Fort Collins perhaps. "When do we leave?"

"Tomorrow."

She blinked. "*This* weekend?"

"Is that a problem?"

"I do have a life outside of this job," she said, not that he'd pick up on the sarcasm.

He cocked his head, eyes glittering in a way she didn't

trust. "What? Hot date?"

"Something like that," she murmured. She hadn't been looking forward to the date anyway, if she were honest.

"You'll have to reschedule."

What would he do if she said *duh*? Ignore her probably. That was his usual reaction to her snarkier comments. She resisted the urge, not wanting a repeat of the tension from earlier.

Leia gave him a small nod. "Of course. What's the purpose of the trip?"

Castor leaned back in his chair. "We'll be attending a mating ceremony, so I assume they have a block of rooms reserved. You'll want to check that."

She lifted her head. "Mating?" That was a new one. They'd traveled to social situations before, mixing business with pleasure. "But I'm only there as your assistant. Correct?"

He crossed his arms, his muscles straining the fine material of his navy suit. "Yes."

Leia didn't like the dark intensity in his eyes, like a storm brewing. Something suspicious lingered there, she just had no idea what it could be. Was it extra dry in here? Where had she left her water bottle? Crap. On her desk. She could really use it about now.

The intensity honed and settled on her as he stood and came around the desk. "The wedding will be under the Banes/Canis names."

She lowered her gaze to make a note, then the names he'd shared sank in and her head snapped up. "No." The word punched out of her.

"What?"

"I'm not going."

Did the sky outside darken? As a son of Zeus, Castor's emotions were sometimes reflected in the weather, but a quick check revealed blue skies outside and his next words were softly put. "Why not?"

"I don't go to wolf-shifter mating ceremonies." Especially not with Castor Dioskouri.

Leia watched with trepidation as Castor leaned back against his desk, ankles crossed, seemingly at total ease. Only somehow she could tell that he was anything but. "Again, why not?" he asked.

She bit her lip but stopped when his gaze automatically dropped to follow the movement. She straightened in her chair, crossing her feet primly at the ankles, knees together. Body language that screamed *keep away*. Which he always had done. The body language was more for herself.

"Have you ever been to a wolf-shifter mating ceremony?" she asked.

"No."

Huh. She would have expected that, in his long lifetime, he would've been to at least one. "Have you heard anything about them?"

He lifted a single eyebrow. "I've been around a while, Lyleia. Of course I've heard."

"So, you know the pair being mated releases a pheromone which makes everyone there very…" She searched for a word appropriate to use with her boss.

"Very?"

She narrowed her eyes at the impatient snap in his voice and tried not to shift in her seat with how her body heated up. "Horny," she bit out.

His eyebrows shot up. "I'm shocked, Ms. Naiad. I wouldn't have expected you to know that word."

"I *am* a nymph," she pointed out drily.

Castor held up his hands. "My apologies. I forget that fact sometimes."

Which firmly put her in her place. Most supernaturals couldn't wait to get with a nymph, for obvious reasons.

The gods had a lot to answer for with that whole giving and receiving pleasure thing. She glanced away, out the window.

"As a nymph, I'd think pheromones shouldn't bother you." Castor's voice dragged her back.

Very carefully, she picked up her computer, stood up, and tucked it into the crook of her arm. "I'm *not* going."

She made it to the door, only to be stopped when he placed his hand over hers on the knob. No whisper of sound reached her ears to warn her of his move, blast his demigod speed. She absorbed the heat of him through her skin, warmth traveling through her blood to pool low.

"I need a reason, Lyleia."

She shivered as the dark, rough tones of his voice made the hairs on the back of her neck stand up. His warm breath brushed over her cheek, his lips only a fraction of space away. What was it about this doorway today?

If she hadn't been so keyed up, she would've laughed at Castor's incredulous irritation. She wondered if the man had ever been denied anything he wanted. Instead, Leia ground her teeth.

Wolf-shifter matings were heady and hedonistic, but he was right—she could handle it under normal circumstances. However, attending one with a demigod who exuded power and sexuality was a different circumstance altogether. That she happened to have a small, apparently uncontrollable, thing for him was a recipe for disaster.

When Delilah had approached her about this job, she'd given one directive: DO NOT FALL FOR HIM.

That was it. Simple enough, to Leia's way of thinking at the time. Delilah was a long-time friend and had known Leia's unique qualifications to resist such a temptation. She'd successfully fended off countless gods and demigods for ages. In the gods' heyday—now referred to as Classical Antiquity, which tickled her sense of humor since it technically made her an antique—the gods had relentlessly pursued her and her sisters and cousins. In addition, Delilah knew Leia's history with gods. She'd picked Leia up, dusted her off, and given her a life.

Leia owed her.

However, given her feelings for him, this mating ceremony was the last place they should be together. She didn't want Castor's last memory of her to be breaking all his rules and throwing herself at him.

"Is it me? You don't trust me?"

She turned her head to face him, taking in his intense blue eyes trained on her in a way that made her want to squirm. His hand still covered hers, the heat of his skin like a brand.

She tipped her chin. "I just…don't like wolf-shifter matings."

His strangely focused expression unsettled her. A heat lit his gaze in a way she'd never seen before, not directed her way at least. Only it couldn't be real. She gave herself a mental slap. *Snap out of it, woman. Wishful thinking gets you nowhere.*

"So, you do trust me?" Something in his voice snagged at her. Like this was important to him.

She swallowed. "I trust you, Castor." Just not herself.

He squeezed her hand. "Good. I don't want to lose you."

She ignored the warmth his statement sent directly to her heart. *He's talking about your work, dummy.*

"And I wouldn't push, but I need you for this," he continued.

If she leaned the tiniest bit forward, she could kiss him. Would his kisses be as electric as everything else about him? Taste like the sky, the way he smelled? Leia swallowed down the crazy urge. "Why?"

He shrugged. "I'm attending to support a good friend on an important day in his life. However, as you've pointed out, things can get a little...interesting...at a wolf-shifter mating. I don't need the complication of sex muddling things up, and you have a unique resistance to me."

"Oh."

"Delilah did an amazing job sending you to me. You've been refreshingly...err...impervious, as well as an excellent assistant."

Leia's heart did a decent impersonation of the Hindenburg, going up in flames as it fell to her feet. He wanted her to go with him because she didn't want him. Message received. She cleared her throat. "Thank you. I think."

He nodded. "I can't go to this alone and risk doing something I'd regret. I'm asking you to protect me from all those raging pheromones. Please."

Damn the man to Hades and back.

He'd asked nicely and given her a reason that meant helping him out in a big way. Her Achilles' heel. Ironically, she'd known the real Achilles well and had mourned his death. The demigod had been a cousin of sorts, his mother Thetis being a sea nymph.

That had been before Leia developed her aversion to the gods.

Leia took a long breath. "Okay."

To give him credit, he didn't gloat. Not that he would. Instead, he looked at her closely, as though gauging her sincerity. "Okay?"

"Yes." She drew her shoulders back. "I'll go make our arrangements now." And then when they got back, she'd resign.

He didn't move away or take his hand from hers. They gazed at each other, neither seemingly willing to break the strangely intimate connection. The freshly spicy scent of him filled her yet again. She'd given him that aftershave for his birthday. Now she was both regretting and savoring the gift.

This has got to stop before we get to the mating.

"May I?" She indicated the door with a jerk of her head.

Slowly, his gaze not leaving her face, Castor stepped back.

With more haste than elegance, she yanked the door open and walked to her desk.

"You're an angel," he called after her.

"Or a sucker," she muttered.

"I heard that."

She dropped into her seat, already regretting agreeing to this. It had disaster written all over it. She needed to leave, go back into hiding, and forget she'd ever worked for Castor Dioskouri.

Chapter Three

Castor shifted, trying to get comfortable in his seat on the private plane Leia had arranged. Shouldn't be hard. He'd designed this plane and it was the lap of luxury. The jet seated ten, operated with a crew of two, and boasted a modern interior—all supple black leather, shining chrome, and that new jet smell.

The constant clack of Leia's fingers on her keyboard sounded ahead of him to the right.

Damn that had been close yesterday. She'd been on the verge of giving him that damn letter of resignation. Again. He'd headed her off only to come a hair's breadth away from losing her anyway, pushing her to accompany him to this wolf-shifter thing.

Castor stared at the side of her face now. She refused to sit with him on flights unless she needed him for what she was working on. The first time they'd traveled together, he'd asked her to move closer.

"Do we have work to get done?" She had looked at him with those wide blue eyes and not even a hint of interest beyond an answer.

A new experience for him.

"No," he'd said slowly.

"Then no thanks." She had given him a half smile that he guessed was meant to soften the blunt words but didn't really help. Then she had turned and plopped into a seat toward the front.

He'd taken his own seat with a lingering sensation of bewilderment and amusement. Women usually threw themselves at him. Granted, he'd asked Delilah for an EA who wouldn't. He just hadn't expected Leia to be quite that... diligent about it.

Now, he read the same paragraph for the fifth time in a row and gave up, closing his own laptop. The plane dropped slightly, and he glanced outside to see mountains not far below. They'd be landing before long.

Leia's typing hadn't slowed. Did the woman ever ease up? She'd shown up at five in the morning for their early flight dressed in her usual neutral—black today—business attire of skirt and top with matching jacket. Not a hair out of place, makeup at a minimum, nails manicured but simple. Not that he could talk, as he was equally formal in a gray, custom-made silk suit, hand-stitched and fitted to perfection. Appearance mattered in the business world.

Still, none of her efforts to play things down could hide her intrinsic beauty. Leia glowed with a loveliness he realized came as much from—maybe more from—the inside as it did the outer wrapping.

A quick glance showed him her arm and the edge of her face, the rest of her blocked by the black leather back of her seat. He studied her quietly—the curve of her cheek, her long dark lashes, her honey blond hair, worn down today, tucked behind her ear. A wicked urge to nibble at the lobe tugged at him, and he adjusted his uncomfortably growing erection as his body responded.

Guilt counteracted the response. Guilt for the idea that maybe he was only pushing his own agenda here. He should just accept her resignation and send her home. Less complicated for both of them.

He took a sip of his coffee—black, strong, bitter...and cold. He made a face. His brain was definitely not engaged today.

Suddenly, Leia swung around. She blinked to find him already watching her but didn't even give him the satisfaction of widened eyes or a blush. Nothing.

Castor raised his eyebrows in question.

"We're coming to the end of the three-month period of support for the Aaron family," she said.

He cleared his throat. "How is Tyler progressing?" He already knew. Jordan Aaron was one of his employees, and his son had leukemia. Castor visited often but kept that from everyone, even Leia.

Her eyes lit up. "He's in full remission."

He nodded as though that was news. "Excellent. Do they need another three months, or should we consider a different need?"

Castor had been covering all the hospital bills for the past six months. Leia had stumbled across his one-man charity for the employees of Dioskouri Enterprises a few months after starting work for him and had asked to help organize it. They selected a different family to help every three months based on needs. But Leia and the families involved were sworn to secrecy.

He didn't need this getting out in the world and ruining his reputation as ruthless and brilliant. Soft was not a descriptor he cultivated. Even if helping in these small ways—to humans or non-humans—gave him a buzz not even designing a new plane could do.

Especially when Leia looked at him like he had a good heart.

She pursed her lips, most likely completely unaware of the impact that one small change in expression did to his cock. "I think," she said, "with the help you've already provided, they are through the worst. Fiona Olline's mother is about to need hospice. I feel there's a greater need there."

Castor waved a hand. "I trust your opinion."

She nodded and turned back to her computer. "Softie McCares-a-Lot," she muttered to herself.

"Share that opinion and you're fired."

The second the words were out he grimaced, then schooled his features to neutral when she turned, as if to assess his seriousness. He raised a single eyebrow and said nothing. After a second she shook her head at him before returning to her work.

He blew out a silent breath.

The thing was, he wanted her to think well of him. That silly muttering made him want to beat his chest and do more good things, just to make her like him. Which was damn ridiculous. Olympus help him, something was going to have to give.

Hence the unaccustomed thoughts bombarding him about this weekend. He'd already planned to bring her. He hadn't been joking when he'd asked for her help. She *was* his buffer at this thing. But then he'd seen that fucking resignation letter and was running out of time.

Now he had a few days to... What? Win her? Seduce her? No...find out if this thing was mutual or not. More importantly, why did she want to leave? Had she realized his changing feelings and this was her way of rejecting him? Leia gave every appearance of loving her work. Happy, satisfied, fulfilled employees were a source of pride for him as a successful businessman. Her plan to leave had triggered a response close to caveman level. He didn't like it.

"Are you challenged?" he asked, his thoughts out of his mouth before he vetted the words first.

Those long, slim fingers paused in their nonstop motion, and she turned in her chair to frown questioningly at him. "Sorry?"

"At work. Are you feeling challenged?" What was wrong with him, blurting it out like that? Usually he was more... subtle.

She blinked at him owlishly, which made him want to shift in his seat like a naughty schoolboy. "Is this about my not wanting to come on the trip?"

"No. This is about your job satisfaction."

Her expression didn't change. If anything, she looked more confused. "Did you know satisfaction in one's job is the number one contributor to personal happiness? They did a study."

He ignored her factoid segue. "Are you?"

"Yes." She drew out the word, obviously not knowing where he was going with the question.

"That doesn't sound sure. Want to rephrase?"

She continued to stare at him with those cobalt blue eyes that seemed to see too much of his soul. "Is there something wrong you're not telling me?"

He cocked his head. "Why?"

"Because you've never asked me a question like that." She shrugged. "I know the business is doing great, but maybe there's a problem with your family? Is Pollux okay?"

And there it was again. A twinge of irrational annoyance—he refused to dub it jealousy—at the idea she might be interested in another man. He'd experienced it twice yesterday. Once with Mike, who'd obviously been hitting on her. The other when he'd realized she'd have to cancel a date this weekend. Now he was suspicious of his own brother. He was losing his mind and his self-control. His attraction to his wife hadn't been nearly this disconcerting.

Get a grip.

He ran a hand over the smooth chrome of his armrest. "Pollux is fine. Answer the question."

She stared at him blankly, a look which he returned with a poker face the pros would envy.

"I love my job."

He couldn't mistake the sincerity in her voice. But why, then, did she want to leave? "Maybe you need more responsibility? Or maybe you want to do something else within the company? Although I'd hate to lose you as an assistant—"

He cut himself off. He was babbling now. He never babbled.

"No." She folded her hands in front of her, and even that gesture had him thinking things he shouldn't. "I'm not exactly shy about speaking up," she said.

He chuckled around the frustrating level of tension building in him. "That's true."

She tossed him another look—concern obvious in her clear eyes—then turned back to her work, effectively dismissing him. He watched her for a bit, battling with the strangest urge to brush her hair away from her neck. Would she lean into his touch or jerk away?

Needing distraction before he embarrassed himself, he reopened his own laptop and tried to read some new contracts until they landed. The nice thing about flying private was how quickly you got out of the airport. Rather than hire a driver, Leia had a rental car waiting for them at the gate. Their luggage was loaded, and they were away within minutes.

At first, they concentrated on getting out of Fort Collins and heading up into the mountains. Eventually they hit a long stretch.

"So…" Leia broke the silence. "Tell me more about this ceremony."

He'd already filled her in on the business deal, a large fleet of private aircraft and vehicles for the new combined wolf pack. "Marrok Banes has been a friend for many years."

"He's the groom?"

He nodded. "Yes, and the alpha for his pack."

"You said Banes/Canis. Weren't their families in a bit of a feud the last hundred years or so?"

He took his gaze off the road for a brief second to send her a surprised glance.

"What? Even nymphs without a spring to their name have a few friends left."

Not many, her tone implied, but he should've figured she'd know something. Nymphs were bound to nature, as were wolf shifters, though in different ways.

"You're correct about their families. The Titans and Gods have nothing on the Banes and Canises." He exaggerated, but not by much. "However, Marrok has been determined to end the feud."

"Let me guess, he's marrying the Canis alpha's daughter?"

"No. The alpha herself."

"Oh!"

Female alphas were rare in the physically dominant wolf shifter world where alphas earned their right to lead, often in bloody ways.

"Does he love her?" was her next question.

"No idea. Knowing Marrok, love didn't enter into the plan. But you could ask Delilah."

She jerked her head to look at him. "She's involved?"

"She introduced the idea to both of them, from what I understand." Apparently, the enigmatic woman could add matchmaker to her list of services.

Leia glanced away, out the passenger-side window.

"Interesting."

He cocked his head at the disdain he detected in her. "Are you a closet romantic, Lyleia?"

No reaction. "You never call me Leia. Why is that?"

A non sequitur, like she often employed with him. She probably thought he used her full name for formality and distance, and that had been true at first. But gradually, that had become his name for her. His. And no one else's. "It's a beautiful name. Your true name," he said. A name and a life she seemed to hide from. "Why won't you look at me? Maybe you are a closet romantic."

"I wasn't *not* looking at you. I was looking at the scenery." She waved a hand at the mountains. They'd left the interstate and were following Highway 36 along the St. Vrain river.

"Your side is solid rock," he pointed out. "The scenery is out my side."

From the corner of his eye, he caught her small movement as she raised her chin.

"I was keeping an eye out for bighorn sheep."

"Sheep," he repeated, not hiding his skepticism.

"Yes. According to my research, they're more common down Big Thompson Canyon, north of here, but have been seen in this area as well. I've never seen one."

He had to give it to his EA...she could bluff with the best of them, but he still wasn't buying it. "Being a romantic isn't a bad thing you know."

"You're an expert on romantics?"

He grunted at the disbelief in her voice. "I was one. A long time ago."

She turned in her seat to face him more fully. "You?"

"Yes, me. I was married, you know."

He waited for the sting of memory that always came when he talked of his wife. But, while the dull ache remained, the bite wasn't harsh anymore. Softer. More bittersweet.

A rare interest lit Leia's eyes. "That was a long time ago, Castor."

No judgment filled her voice. More...concern. For him?

"I loved her deeply. We were childhood sweethearts. After she died, I never expected to love like that again, and I haven't." Now why had he confessed that? He never talked about Hilaera. Maybe the similarity between his wife and his feelings for Leia now, though the two women had nothing in common, had him thinking more of that time.

Leia was quiet for a long stretch of road. "Do you miss her?" she asked, her tone noticeably gentler.

He could have given a trite answer, but he didn't want to. "Every day."

She fiddled with her hands in her lap. "Are you lonely?"

"I've managed to keep occupied." He tightened his grip on the wheel. He didn't want her pity.

"I just...don't like the idea of you lonely."

His eyebrows shot up.

She rushed to explain, stumbling over her words. "It seems wrong. For someone immortal. Someone so strong. You know?"

He grunted a reply, thinking over her words. "I get the feeling you're just as lonely."

That wiped every emotion from her face in one fell swoop, automation taking over. "I've always been happier on my own."

Castor hid a sigh. *Damn.*

Chapter Four

The rest of the drive didn't take too long. Probably a good thing for his sanity and a raging erection, thanks to the spring rain scent of the woman sitting beside him.

He'd never been turned on by a simple smell before. These days it happened all the damn time.

"Now *there* is a hotel worth staying at. Your friend has good taste in wedding venues." Leia made the comment as Castor drove them through the town of Estes Park to the Stanley.

The hotel sat up above a shopping center, high enough that you could see all the buildings. The front faced downtown Estes Park. Mountains rose up around them like a cathedral of granite. The hotel itself was stunning—Victorian in style, white with red tile roofs, stark against the darker colors of rock and pine trees.

Rather than valet, they parked and walked their suitcases in. Despite his power, his money, and everything else going for him, Castor still preferred to do most things himself.

"I'll take that." He held out his hand for Leia's luggage.

"No, you won't." She pulled out the handle and started rolling it to the building.

Castor shook his head at her independent streak but didn't argue and followed in silence. They made their way up a set of stairs to a large porch covered with white wicker chairs to enjoy the view. Several double doors leading into the reception area were thrown wide, letting in the brisk May breeze, carrying with it the crisp scent of pine trees.

Once inside, the receptionist at the hotel had a surprise for them both.

"Mr. Banes did what?" Leia squeaked beside Castor.

The woman's smile wavered. "He placed you in the suite beside theirs."

"A single room?" Leia asked for clarification.

"It's a suite, but yes."

She turned to Castor. "You take the suite. It's obviously meant for the guest of honor." No surprise a demigod at the ceremony would have garnered attention. "I'll get another room."

"We don't have any more rooms available." The receptionist gave them an apologetic grimace. "And I doubt you'll find anything anywhere else. There's a horror film festival going on this week."

Oddly appropriate. Castor just kept from pulling a face in front of Leia who was visibly freaking out. Her knuckles turned white as she crushed the nice brochure she'd plucked from a holder on the desk when they'd been waiting in line.

Castor covered her hand with his. "Don't worry about it."

"Don't—" She bit down on the words when she turned and recognized the warning he was trying to silently communicate with his eyes.

"Let's get settled. Then we'll figure it out."

Her lips were pale as she clenched her teeth, but she gave him a jerky nod. After they got their keys, she followed him without a word. Their suitcases made a *clack-clack-clack* as they crossed the lobby with its original wood floors. They passed large fireplaces with comfy seating around them, then headed up the grand staircase covered in a deep maroon velvet carpet.

"I can't stay here with you," she said as soon as they got to their room and the door closed behind them. "I'll get a hotel room down in Denver or Fort Collins if I have to." She crossed to the mini fridge in the corner and pulled out a bottled water, which she proceeded to gulp down. Never a good sign when Leia needed to chug water.

The woman always had a bottle with her, but he'd just assumed she was being healthy. Until the first time she'd downed three bottles in front of him in rapid succession. That had been the day his brother showed up at the office with their father in tow. If looks could kill, Zeus would've been toast.

Guilt pressing on him—he'd fucking put her in this position—Castor shook his head. "There are too many events, and I don't want you driving the canyons at night. I'll sleep on the couch."

She glanced at the couch in the sitting room, a piece deliberately created to imitate an old-fashioned sofa, with the scrolling back and armrests in wood, and the cushions in a patterned, pink silk. Then she moved her pointed gaze to him, eyeballing his six-foot-three frame. Like every demigod, his body was built for battle.

She shook her head. "*I'll* sleep on the couch."

But he didn't like that option, either. Having Leia on the uncomfortable piece of furniture didn't sit right with him. Before he could offer another suggestion, the phone rang.

He held up a finger and crossed the room to answer it.

"How do you like the suite?" Marrok asked after they exchanged hellos.

"Thank you for the upgrade." He caught Leia's wrinkled nose from the corner of his eye and had to bite back a laugh. What else was he supposed to say?

"My pleasure. Thank you for agreeing to stand up for me on the big day."

Castor glanced at Leia in case she'd caught that. He hadn't warned her about his role in the ceremony, yet. But she'd stopped paying attention to him. Instead, she'd started unpacking and hanging her garments in the closet. He took the opportunity to appreciate how her black skirt highlighted her lovely backside. She'd removed her jacket, allowing him to see her hourglass figure better. He fucking adored those pencil skirts she favored.

"Castor?"

He pulled his attention back to the conversation. "Absolutely, buddy."

"Tala and I would like to have lunch with you and your date today."

Castor glanced at his watch. "What time were you thinking?"

"Noon."

An hour to convince Leia might be enough. "Sounds good."

"We'll meet you in the lobby."

Castor hung up and turned, conjuring up his most winning smile. Though, he used it so rarely, it felt more like a crack breaking concrete on his face.

She turned from the closet, paused at the sight of him, and crossed her arms. "Don't even bother with that smile, Castor Dioskouri."

He blinked and snapped his mouth closed, swallowing the words on the tip of his tongue.

"I heard," she said.

"I see."

She nodded. "Give me a half hour to wash off the travel and change. More casual for lunch with a friend, I assume?"

"Probably a good idea."

She pulled a dress from the closet where she'd just finished hanging it. He stayed where he was as she gathered other things and crossed the room.

"By the way…"

Her voice pulled him out of his head, which had gone on ahead to her naked in the shower. Where the hell had his control disappeared to? Now she stared at him from the doorway to the bathroom.

He raised his eyebrows in question.

"Congrats on being the best man at the ceremony." The woman actually winked before she closed the door behind her.

I am never going to figure her out. And that was half the fun.

Chapter Five

"You should probably know this mating is not an easy one." Castor tossed the words in her general direction as they crossed the lobby of the hotel.

She kept the pleasant smile plastered to her lips despite the desire to glare at the man beside her. "Delilah's involvement and it being an arranged mating was a pretty strong clue," she muttered between clenched teeth. "But what else haven't you told me?"

Her frustrating boss flashed another smile. Two in one day had to be a record. This one, she figured, was only meant to buy him acquiescence. "Great dress by the way," he said.

While she did like the knee-length, blush-colored dress with a sweet belt tied in a bow at her waist, he wasn't going to distract her. "Thank you, but you're not off the hook."

"Too late, they're right over there." He put one hand to her back while he raised the other to catch his friend's attention. "Marrok."

The wolf couple was waiting for them in white wicker chairs on the large porch at the front of the hotel. Leia was glad she'd changed, as both were dressed casually. Like Castor, Marrok wore jeans and a button-up with the long sleeves rolled back. Tala Canis wore a stylish single-piece pantsuit in a striking blue. They appeared to be deep in serious conversation until Castor hailed them. They stood, and Leia noted both were tall and lean, typical build for wolf shifters.

After the two men shook hands, Marrok introduced his bride-to-be. The male wolf's voice had a dark rasp to it, like a rumbling growl. Deep laugh lines around his eyes spoke of an inherent kindness. She decided she liked him.

"Congratulations on your upcoming mating." Leia offered her felicitation to them both.

Behind Tala's shoulder, an older woman did a double take, probably at Leia's word choice. Damn. She'd have to remember they were among humans here.

Marrok simply nodded. Deep blue eyes gazed back at her from under thick black eyebrows. He had silver at his temples, not unusual for an alpha, even a relatively young one. She placed his age around thirty-two.

The small smile she received from Tala was shadowed by a wariness in the elegant blonde's stunning green eyes. Castor had said this wasn't a love match, but was the bride reluctant?

"I'm surprised the dragon shifters in the area didn't have something to say about it," she said. "Isn't the Alliance headquarters close to here?"

From what she understood, the kings and clans had established colonies in the Americas, and the Alliance were their trusted men who ruled in their stead.

"Farther north," Marrok confirmed. "We have a—" He glanced at Tala who rolled her eyes. "Let's just say we have a truce of sorts. We don't get involved in their stuff, and they leave us the hell alone. Not that they care about wolf shifters."

Interesting.

"How long have you two been dating?" Tala asked with a polite smile.

Castor turned to Leia, his hand at her back again, warm through the thin silk of her dress. She resisted the urge to lean into that hand and straightened away from him instead, then shot him a pointed look.

Resisting the man was supposed to be part of her job. Dammit.

He cleared his throat. "Lyleia is my executive assistant."

"An office romance? That's new for you, old man," Marrok teased.

"I'm not his date," Leia explained tightly. "Just his camouflage."

Marrok looked back at Leia with a grimace. "I hope my changing your rooms to a suite isn't an issue, Lyleia?"

She gave him a serene smile. "Call me Leia, please. Everyone else does. And not at all. I'm a nymph, which means I have a natural resistance to demigods."

If only *she* could remember that fact. Especially through the ceremony.

"Oh really?" Marrok's drawl cut through Castor's warning grunt.

She tipped her head up. "Of course. In fact, it's why I was hired to be his assistant. Dark, movie-star good looks, brooding personality, and adorable though rarely sighted dimples do nothing for me whatsoever." She gave Castor's arm a patronizing pat even as she lied through her teeth.

His eyebrows winged high. "You think my dimples are adorable?"

She rolled her eyes. "You *would* only pay attention to that part." She turned back to the other couple, who'd watched the exchange with wide-eyed interest. "Shall we?"

At least that got them moving. Marrok led them outside and around to the valet parking. "It was a good idea to bring a shield to the ceremony."

"The unclaimed women will be naturally drawn to his power during the ceremony," Tala murmured. "He'll have to beat them off with a two-by-four even with you there."

"So now I'm a giant bat?" She shook her head at Castor who just shrugged. "I think I need a raise."

They got into a sleek gray Jaguar sedan with Marrok behind the wheel. The wolves' scents, which had been subtler in the open air, swirled around them, reminding Leia of warm days in fresh plowed fields of fertile black earth, like the land close to her spring in Greece. She inhaled appreciatively, giving a small hum of contentment, muscles letting go of tension despite herself. "You smell like home."

Beside her Castor gave a small jerk. No wonder, as Leia never talked about her life before.

Tala turned from her seat in the front. "Most people say we smell like dirt. Or wet dog."

Leia shook her head. "I like it."

"You said you're a nymph?" the other woman asked, only mildly curious.

"I was." Five hundred years of facing that harsh reality gave her the strength to keep the tremor out of her voice. "My spring was buried under lava and destroyed." *Thanks to a werewolf.* Tala and Marrok's ancestors.

She kept that last part to herself.

"I see. I'm sorry," Tala murmured.

An off tone to Tala's voice caught Leia's attention and she cocked her head as Tala and Marrok exchanged an odd glance. "Have you met a nymph before?"

"No. But your gifts having me thinking." Tala turned in her seat, eyeing Leia as though sizing her up. "I wonder if you might be able to help us."

Leia was hard-pressed to think of what a nymph could do for a wolf. "I'd be happy to, if I can. What do you need?"

Tala and Marrok exchanged another glance. "In order to explain that, let me fill you in on the reasons behind our mating first," Tala said.

"Okay."

"Marrok and I are the alphas of our packs."

"Castor told me. I know female alphas are rare. I've never heard of two alphas mating. Is it common?"

"Our union is…highly unusual," Marrok said.

Tala's lips thinned in a grim line. "Our packs have been ripping out each other's jugulars for centuries. Marrok and I see this mating as an opportunity to end that fighting."

Leia could appreciate the goal, but these two had a tough road ahead. "Who will be alpha of the combined pack? If you don't mind my asking."

"We will lead together," Marrok said.

Tala's lips tightened though. "As you can guess, there are factions within both packs against our mating."

Made sense. A feud lasting that long didn't die a quick death. "I fail to see how a nymph could help."

Marrok parked the car in a crowded lot downtown where they were going for lunch, but instead of getting out, he turned in his seat. "I believe my intended is thinking that a sign of blessing from the gods might help."

Leia glanced back and forth between them, still not following.

"A sign along the lines of a display of nature," Tala added.

Oh… Oh, shit. Nature.

Of all supernatural creatures, nymphs were perhaps the most tied to nature, to the point that she could manipulate water with ease. Or she'd been able to once upon a time. These days she didn't get close enough to larger bodies of it to try.

"You want me to help put on a show?" she asked slowly while cringing inside.

"Maybe you could recruit other nymphs in the area?" Marrok suggested. "The chapel is set in the mountains all by itself, surrounded by nature."

Castor said nothing. She wasn't entirely sure what Delilah had told him, but why did he suddenly feel closer, his heat nearer? As if he was ready to jump between her and pain if he could. But he couldn't.

She dropped her gaze to her hands clenched in her lap. Working for Castor had been a big risk. She'd thought that, after all this time, she'd be okay poking her head up, but that was already in doubt if what she'd been sensing was correct. Showing her face to members of her extended family would make it harder to disappear. "I don't think that's a good idea."

"Why?" Tala asked.

After ages of practice, she was able to keep the pain that still ripped through her out of her voice, even if her hands shook. "I lost my spring and was shunned. Treated as a disease among them to be quarantined and cut out as quickly as possible." Until she'd faked her own death and walked away from everything she knew.

Castor must have caught a trace of how shattered she still was, though, because he reached over to cover her hands with his. "I didn't know that."

She cast him a quick glance. "Why do you think I needed a job as your EA instead of guarding a spring?"

The warmth of Castor's hand on hers and his silent support seeped into her, his strength warming her soul from the inside out. Thawing places she'd long thought frozen inside her.

She pulled her shoulders back and raised her gaze from her lap to the couple seated before her. A couple putting aside their personal needs to bring peace to their people. Their cause was worth her pride; she'd focus on that, rather than her pathetic little story. She was a stronger woman because of her past, dammit. Time to start acting like it.

"This is important?" she asked.

Tala grimaced. "It could be a huge help. Put to rest some of the doubts long enough for us to unite and settle the packs..." She trailed off.

"We wouldn't ask, but..." Marrok also trailed off.

"I will try. That's all I can promise."

Tala reached over the seat and patted Leia's knee. "Thank you."

Leia tried to smile, though it felt stiff. There was no way this would go well.

Chapter Six

After a quick lunch in a busy bistro downtown, a little too close to the river for Leia's comfort, Tala and Marrok brought them to the location for the mating ceremony. The idea was to give Leia a chance to try to approach the nymphs nearby in privacy, rather than waiting until the night of the mating.

Wow. They hadn't been kidding about being in the middle of nature.

The idyllic chapel Tala and Marrok had selected for the marriage ceremony was positioned on top of a large rock base, built of the same granite, almost as though it had been placed there since the beginning of time, forged by the gods themselves. Below, a creek-fed lake reflected the blues of the sky and the spire of the chapel.

Such a gorgeous setting was perfect for this event. After a human-style wedding ceremony, Marrok's and Tala's family and friends would follow them into the wooded mountainside for the mating ceremony and celebrations illuminated by the full moon, followed by a more formal reception held at the Stanley Hotel, where they were staying.

Her skin crackled with energy just being here. Part of hiding had been staying in cities and avoiding open country. Leia could sense the nymphs nearby, even from the car in the parking lot.

An oread nymph of mountains and grottos guarded the nearest peak. A melissae nymph protected her precious honeybees in the field of flowers, along with the anthousai flower nymph, beyond the pond. A dryades wood nymph watched over the deeper woods. While a potameides river nymph controlled the rapids, a naiad water nymph, like her, kept the pond pristine. She would approach that sister and hope for a favorable response. Hope was all she had. She'd stopped praying to the gods long ago.

Castor reached over and threaded his fingers with hers, calling her attention to how she'd been wringing her hands. It was the second time he'd touched her like this, and she was starting to like it. Too much. "Do you want me to come with you?"

Not really. "Remind me to contact Mike when we get back. I forgot to get him started on the Brockway account."

"Lyleia?" Castor prompted, voice going quiet. "That was a yes or no question."

She heaved an inward sigh. The nymphs might be more likely to listen to a demigod than to her. While they had the ability to resist a god, most nymphs didn't bother. They were attracted to the power the same as many other creatures. Him being a son of Zeus would only amplify their interest.

"Yes." Decision made, she hopped out of the car. Time to get this over with.

One thing Castor was good at was shutting up when he needed to. In silence, he followed her down around the chapel to where the creek met the lake. At the edge of the water, not quite touching, she paused and closed her eyes, absorbing the energy swirling around her this close to fresh water.

She breathed in the pure scent of it, her skin tingling with vitality. The gods knew she missed this. Crouching down, she waved her hand over the surface of the river, not touching. That would be rude.

"Sister." She whispered the word.

No response.

"Sister. Will you speak with me?"

She braced herself for silent rejection, or worse, some form of denouncement. What she wasn't ready for was a dripping wet woman, clothed in a diaphanous white gown, to launch herself out of the river and wrap her arms around Leia's neck, soaking her from head to toe.

"Leia!" the nymph squealed.

Leia held up a hand to hold off Castor, who'd stepped forward, hands fisting, obviously confused by the scene. "Hello, Calliadne." Leia pulled back to smile at her sister.

Only to blink at the sight of tears. Calli shook her head, her eyes wide with shock. "By the gods, how are you alive? I thought you died centuries ago. Without your spring..."

Without her spring and shunned by her people. It hadn't been easy. "I didn't know you'd relocated," she said.

The adorable redhead—now dry as a bone and perfectly coifed and made up, a trick Leia continued to use every time she got out of the shower and employed now to her bedraggled form—waved a dismissive hand. "The Nile was getting too crowded with all my father's offspring." Nilus was a minor god of that river, and prolific with children. "I much prefer this lovely place. So peaceful." Her blue eyes turned grayer and she flicked little nervous glances around. "But, Lyleia, as much as my heart sings to see you again, you need to leave. Quickly." She shivered as wind whipped through the nearby aspen grove, shaking the leaves like rattlesnake rattles.

Not good.

"I love you," Calli continued, "but nothing has changed.

We were told never to associate with you or there would be consequences."

Leia's lips flattened as she breathed her anger through her nose. "A long time ago, and that person is surely dead by now."

Calli bit her lip. "Maybe…"

"I said no to a god, and he buried my spring under a river of lava." Out of the corner of her eye, she caught Castor's twitchy movement in reaction to her words. She ignored him. "And no one did anything to help me."

Calli grimaced. "I know." She flicked a glance toward Castor. "I'm surprised you're here with a demigod."

"I'm his executive assistant."

"Lucky you." Calli shot a sassy wink at Castor who, in turn, sent Leia a confounded look.

Leia tried not to grind her teeth and talked quickly. "We're here for a wolf-shifter mating ceremony and I could use your help. *All* the nymphs' help."

The water in the river started to gurgle and ripple as it flowed faster. Calli shifted nervously. "I don't think—"

A breeze swept through the trees in a *shoosh* of pine needles. The nymphs in the area certainly were stirred up by Leia's presence among them, a fact that, even after all this time, wrapped around her heart and threatened to crush it. "Will you meet me later?"

Calli stepped back, face stiff. "You have to go. They're holding back because it's you."

The gurgling changed to a rush, and the water was pouring in and pooling. Leia stepped back as well, careful to keep her feet dry. "In town at the Stanley Hotel. Please, Calli?"

Another gust of wind and burble of the water, and Calli stiffened visibly. "I can't. I'm sorry."

Leia reached out and squeezed her sister's hand, even as

her own heart broke all over again. "I understand."

She backed up to find Castor glaring at the water and the woods with a dark scowl. She tugged on his elbow. "Let's go." He didn't move. Another tug. "Castor."

Those intense blue eyes—offended on her behalf, which only made her like him more—shifted to her face. "Yes."

He placed his hand at the small of her back, that one gesture lending her the strength she needed to walk back to the car with her head held high. She wasn't afraid, just sad. After all this time, she'd hoped...

She got in the back. Tala and Marrok, who wouldn't have had a full view of what had gone on but couldn't have failed to notice the strange water and wind activity, stared at her, a hundred questions in their eyes.

"They won't help."

Tala and Marrok visibly drooped. Then Tala offered her a small smile. "It was worth a try. Before you showed up, we didn't have a plan at all beyond mating, so now we're back to that."

"Maybe. I think I have a plan." Of sorts. Leia hadn't expected to win the other nymphs to her side, but their fear was irrational and wrong. What if what happened to her happened to another of her kind, someone not strong enough to survive it? Maybe it was beyond time for her to make a statement of her own to her so-called family...and help Tala and Marrok in the process.

The drive back to the hotel was a quiet one, and they said their goodbyes in the foyer. As soon as they got to their room, Leia snagged a chilled water from the fridge and collapsed on the couch. A long gulp had her feeling marginally improved. A bath would be even better. Not as good as a fresh spring, but that would never be an option.

She closed her eyes, struggling with the weight of her failure and her loneliness. Usually she could put it to the back of her mind. Focus on work.

"Are you going to explain what happened back there?"

Damn. She'd almost forgotten the glowering demigod in the room who had been dead silent all the way back. She didn't bother to open her eyes. "I'm not particularly in the mood for a postmortem right now."

Her eyes popped open when he scooped her up in his arms, then proceeded to sit back down, cradling her in his lap. Where she shouldn't be, except he felt so good against her. Comforting even as that damn chemical reaction kicked in and heat swamped her senses.

"Why would the other nymphs be mad at you?" he asked, quietly now, though she could tell he was holding back for her sake. His arms were rigid around her.

She sighed, tempted to lay her head and all her problems on his shoulders. Instead she traced the fine material of his shirt collar, careful not to touch skin, no matter how tempting. "Did you know the term nymphomaniac—"

"Lyleia." The soft word had a growly edge to it, cutting off her attempt at distraction.

She sighed. "Not mad. Afraid."

"Why?"

"I'm not entirely sure. I used to think that they simply feared what happened to me. Gods aren't always good news for us. We're also a superstitious lot and fear another's misfortune will be visited on us. But the way Calli worded it…" As though someone had directly threatened the nymphs. She shook her head. It had been bothering her all the way back to the hotel.

"That's family for you," he muttered.

"Yeah." She huffed a laugh, surprised she could.

"Which god?"

"Poseidon."

Though he'd been tricked into it by a werewolf. More

ancient than wolf shifters who descended from them, werewolves were not only older but larger and more powerful. And this one had been a full-on asshole megalomaniac.

Granted, publicly humiliating him had been a damn idiotic idea on her part. But he hadn't given her much choice.

She'd believed he was dead until those two break-ins at her apartment. If he wasn't, did she dare risk his wrath again with what she was planning to do?

Castor's arms relaxed against her. Realizing she still clutched the water bottle in one hand, she took another swig, feeling infinitely better, though whether the water or Castor was the cause she couldn't say for sure.

"At least it wasn't Zeus," he said finally.

What would he do if she pressed a kiss to the column of his throat? Probably dump her on her ass. "I would've refused to work for you had it been Zeus."

"I'm actually surprised Poseidon would punish you by demolishing your spring. He loves water nymphs."

"He loves oceanids, not naiads." She lifted one shoulder. "A god scorned, and all that. He had Hephaestus do the dirty work."

His thumb moved against her hip, tracing lazy circles that were beyond distracting, especially when she found herself relaxing into the touch. "I'm sorry," he murmured.

She could get addicted to his touch. Time to run. The second she pushed against his hold, Castor released her, and she hopped up.

"I need a bath." She'd made it to the door when his voice stopped her.

"What did Calli mean when she said, *they're holding back because of you*?"

She glanced over her shoulder, taking in his serious expression, and managed a smile. "I was pretty powerful, once upon a time. Maybe they were scared to test me."

He studied her for a long moment. "I'm not buying it."

She crossed her arms. "That I was powerful?"

"That your power had anything to do with them holding back. I think they genuinely liked you in that once upon a time you mention, and that keeps them from unleashing on you now."

Hurt pooled in her gut, turning her insides to stone faster than a look from Medusa. This was too painful to talk about. She cleared her throat. "I doubt it."

"Why not? *I* like you." His gaze changed from serious to molten in a blink, stealing the air from the room and replacing it with thick, urgent need.

Definitely time to run before she did something stupid like tackle him and beg him to help her forget, if just for a little while. "Yeah…well. The feeling's mutual."

Damn. Where had that come from? Run, stupid.

She fled into the bathroom, locking the door behind her. A nice long soak would bring her back to her senses and empower her for her chat with Calli later. Something was definitely off with her sisters. She just couldn't put her finger on what.

Chapter Seven

Leia needed to not be cooped. The room was stifling her. Instead, she spent a good deal of time wandering the grounds of the hotel, enjoying the cool breeze and the smells of the mountains, until it got dark.

All the while, she worked through what she intended to do at the ceremony. It wouldn't win her any popularity points with her sister nymphs, but they'd ousted her from their circle anyway. Had they even mourned her death? Was she angry enough with them to force a confrontation?

Yeah. None of what happened to her was her fault, dammit. Maybe if they'd stood with her...

Feet heavy with her thoughts, she trudged up the stairs and through the doors into the foyer of the main hotel building.

"Everything okay?" Castor's voice had her swinging her gaze sharply right as she walked in.

She frowned to find him lounging in one of the big leather chairs close to a big stone fireplace in the lobby, a cheerful fire crackling away, giving off a comforting campfire odor.

While the early May days were warm enough, the nights were still crisply chilly, which was why she'd added a long brown sweater over her pink dress and changed out her heels for a pair of tall suede boots. "Were you waiting for me?"

He held up a leather-bound book, *The Shining*. "Nope."

She moved closer, took the book from him, careful not to touch his fingers as she did, and flipped through the pages. "Creep-tastic."

His mouth tilted up on one side. "It seemed appropriate, given the surroundings."

She gave a hum of agreement. "You know this place is haunted, right?"

Castor tilted his head, studying her closely, something in his gaze she didn't quite trust. "You believe in ghosts?"

She ignored the second comment—or tried to—then shrugged and handed the book back. "I know a couple ghosts, actually."

"I guess you do then."

She thumbed over her shoulder toward the stairs. "I'm going to our room now. Are you going to stay down here?"

He unfolded his long length from the overstuffed chair. "I'll come up with you."

Leia glanced over his shoulder as she nodded, and froze, her entire body going rigid with shock and screaming fear.

"Lyleia?" Castor's voice brought her back to herself.

As she unfroze, her flight instinct kicked in hard. With a gasp, she ducked, then leaned over, peeking around Castor's bulk, focused on a man laughing with a group of five or six other men. Kaios. The werewolf was still drop-dead handsome, still remarkably young looking for one so old. She'd bet money he was also still the same total and utter ass.

Her mind rattled with thoughts that she couldn't quite piece together...

He was supposed to be dead.

The instinct that told her someone had broken into her apartment, twice, might have been right.

No way was it a coincidence that he appeared here now.

"Shit," she hissed through clenched teeth. Anger disappeared as panic flipped her heart rate to max. She frantically scanned the room for an escape. Seeing none close enough, she stepped closer to Castor, practically burrowing into him, letting his size hide her.

"What the—" Castor glanced over his shoulder at whatever had captured her attention.

She yanked on his arm. "Don't look," she whispered. Werewolves had terrific hearing.

Castor whipped his head around only to stare down at her, his gaze almost comically a combination of worried and stunned at her behavior. "What's going on?"

She peeped around her demigod shield. *Crap.* Kaios was walking this way. He'd see her any second. She glanced up at Castor, who stared at her like she'd lost her mind. Because she had.

"Kiss me," she demanded.

His eyebrows shot up. "Excuse me?"

"You heard me." Only a few more seconds.

He shook his head. "You want me to—"

"Screw it," she muttered.

Going up on tiptoe, she wrapped her arms around his neck, pulling him down to her. Taken by surprise, he didn't resist as she covered his lips with hers.

Castor stiffened against her, going totally unresponsive at first, which didn't matter because she was more occupied with where her nemesis was in the room. But then he took over—large hands flat against her back, pressing her body closer to his, lips warm and so insistent that she went from distracted to completely and utterly focused…on Castor.

Electricity sizzled through her body, her nerves coming

to glorious life at his every touch, starting from what his lips were doing, then spreading outward. Those lips, warm against her own—they mastered, they coaxed, they tempted and teased. She gave a small moan as he ran his tongue along the seam of her lips only to tangle with hers, brush against hers, when she opened to him on a whimper. His hands smoothed under her sweater, over her back to her hips, where he used a light grip to tug her in closer to his body, the ridge of his erection pressing into her belly.

For a demigod he was amazingly gentle. A warm glow of rightness joined the heat of passion. In his arms was where she was meant to be.

Wrong. Wrong. Wrong.

The warning bells went off in her head. This was her boss. And a demigod. And a man who desperately wanted to avoid sexual complications and messy emotions. Nothing was right about this.

And she needed to run. Far and fast. Disappear.

With a different gasp, this one mortification, she jerked back, stepping out of Castor's arms before he could stop her. Her hand flew to her lips, which throbbed from his touch. Oh, great gods, she'd just kissed her boss like the nymph she'd once been.

He pinned her with blazing blue eyes, skin tight across his cheekbones and around his eyes. "Wow." His voice was low and raspy and skittered along her nerves in a delicious way.

A quick glance showed Kaios had left the room. Thank the gods.

She pulled her shoulders back. Time to act casual. "Thanks for helping me with that. I'm sorry if it got out of hand. I couldn't think of any other way to avoid that son of a hellhound."

Passion shifted to confusion as his brows lowered in a

glower. "Helping you with *what*?"

Leia blinked at the sudden change. He'd only been playing along…hadn't he? "I was hiding from someone. I thought you realized."

She checked over her shoulder, belatedly. There was no sign of her tormentor, thank the gods.

A quick glance back at Castor revealed an angry scowl on his face. "Let's go," he said. Or ordered.

He took her by the elbow, but a flash of pink on the floor caught her eye. When had he untied her belt? She snatched it up and cast Castor a glower of her own, daring him to say a word. Head held high, she led the way.

As soon as they were in the suite, she beelined straight for the bathroom. A long soak in water was what she needed right now.

"Hey."

She paused in the doorway and glanced over her shoulder at him in the main room, his eyebrows raised in question. Bluffing her way through this was her best bet.

He crossed his arms, and she did her best to ignore how the muscles strained the fine material of his shirt or the strength of his forearms exposed by his rolled-back sleeves.

"You're going to explain what happened down there."

Damn. She'd hoped he'd let it go. Time to play dumb. "Um. I saw a person I'd rather avoid. You helped me avoid him."

She turned away.

"Hold on, you."

She gave a little sigh before she turned back around, then yelped because he'd managed to cross the room to stand directly behind her without a sound.

She blinked up at him. "What?"

"You're telling me that kiss was all an act?"

That panty-melting, set-me-on-fire, take-me-now kiss?

Men could be so dense. "Of course." She grimaced. "I shouldn't have kissed you at all, but he showed up and I just kind of…panicked."

He put his hands on the doorframe on either side of her, leaning close, his fresh-air scent swirling around her, casting her more under his thrall, and she found she couldn't pull her gaze away. So, Leia did the next best thing. She hardened her heart and held her ground, angling her head to look him in the eyes.

"So if I were to kiss you right now"—his gaze dropped to her lips, making her tingle as though he'd already put words into action—"you'd feel nothing?"

Ah. That's his problem. She'd pricked his pride. Shoving aside her unreasonable disappointment, she tried to forget the utterly perfect feel of his lips against hers. "Of course I'd feel something. I'm a nymph and you're a demigod." And a hell of a kisser. And she had this uncontrollable thing for him. "But it wouldn't mean anything. You're my boss, not my lover."

He gave her a long, hard look, and a sound of splintering wood told her he'd gripped the doorframe a tad too hard, though she didn't check to confirm. Her stomach tightened when his gaze dropped to her lips again and he seemed to lean closer.

Leia held very still. Waiting. Wishing…

But then he stepped back. "You're right."

Disappointment mingled with relief as her pent-up breath punched from her. "It won't happen again."

That statement didn't make her feel any better. Regret dragged her heart down to the pit of her stomach.

"Who were you trying to avoid?"

She tipped her chin. "I'd rather not talk about it."

"Too bad."

She knew the stubborn light in his eyes, his jaw clenched

with determination. He'd get it out of her by hook or by crook. "The werewolf responsible for losing me my spring."

His eyes narrowed. "You told me Poseidon was responsible."

"Yes, but it started with Kaios. He wanted me. I rejected him." She left out the details on purpose. "To get even, he made a bet with Poseidon that the god would also fail with me. If he lost, Kaios was supposed to bring the god something. I never did find out what. If Kaios won, Poseidon would punish me much more than Kaios ever could."

She gazed out the window at the lights of the shopping center below the hotel and the cars driving to and from the downtown area. "He must be here for the mating. Having an ancient like Kaios here to bless the mating with their presence is desired by the wolves. Except…I wasn't aware he was still alive."

They tended to die faster than other immortals given their proclivity toward fighting each other and the world, and she'd avoided everything werewolf since the day her spring had been destroyed. Until now.

Kaios was a self-centered megalomaniac, though. No way was the guy here to bless a mating. It couldn't be coincidence. But he couldn't be here for her, right? Yes, she'd rejected him. Granted, the way she'd gone about it—close to drowning him with the water from a river in a show of how her power could trump his, to get him to back off, and doing so in front of the most powerful of his people—had been beyond stupid. But he couldn't still hold a grudge. Could he?

Castor was silent for so long, she glanced back up. Her eyes widened at the expression on his face, a mixture of guilt and tender protectiveness. But that couldn't be right.

Before she could say anything, he took her face in his hands. "Don't go."

She blinked as her heart pulsed. "What?"

"Don't go to the mating ceremony. Go home. I'll deal with things here."

She bit her lip. "What about Marrok and Tala?"

"When I explain things to them, they'll understand that you couldn't stay," he said softly.

The thing was, no way could she back down now. She may have hidden in the foyer, but something inside her cried out in protest.

She hadn't resigned for a reason. Because she'd be leaving the only happiness she'd found in a long, long time—Castor and her job. Just to escape the worry that she'd be found.

No.

A big, fucking no.

She'd let Kaios do too much to control her life, even when she'd thought him dead and gone. No more. Leaving, running and hiding, meant Kaios would win. Again.

She swallowed. "No. A werewolf at their mating is a big deal to them. Don't say anything to them."

"Then I'll tell them you're sick or something. I'm not going to put you through facing your own personal demon. Not for me." His eyes darkened, turning the color of a storm. Any second now, lightning would flash.

This was why she was unable to resist him. Castor Dioskouri was an intrinsically good man who put others before his own needs, despite being a demigod.

She covered his hands with her own, leaning into the heat of him. "I want to stay. I'm going to help them, and Kaios can be damned to the lowest pits of Hades."

With a groan Castor released her face only to pull her into this body and wrap his arms around her. He settled his chin on the top of her head. Leia closed her eyes, reveling in the sensation of being surrounded by him, giving in to her own weakness. Just for a second. "You have a good heart, Lyleia Naiad. Why help people you've only just met?"

Because they were Castor's friends, only she couldn't tell him that. "Because you think they are good, and their goal of bringing peace to their packs is a worthy one. And I'm sick to death of running."

He grunted. "What's your plan?"

She scrunched up her face. "If I told you, you wouldn't let me do it."

He moved his hands to her shoulders to lean back and look her in the eyes, frowning. "Which means it's dangerous."

"Not necessarily dangerous. More like…"

"Stupid?"

Usually a term like that would earn him a verbal smack down, but he was worried about her, so she let it pass. "I've been called worse. I'll be fine."

"I can't talk you out of this, can I?"

"No. It's been so long since I've had a chance to use my powers at all, let alone for a good cause. I'm not asking you, Castor. I'm telling you. I *want* to do this."

To feel some worth. To access the elements again. Maybe show her sisters that by abandoning her they were complicit in her fate. And show a certain werewolf that she was done.

"Do you need to be at the mating ceremony for it to work?" She could see his mind ticking over, trying to make a solution that fit his determination to protect her.

"It's better if I am. I need to be close by."

"Which means you'll have to come face to face with Kaios." His lips flattened in a grim line her fingers itched to smooth over.

She held onto his hands tighter. "I'll handle him." With Castor there, she knew she could.

Castor's eyebrow hitched. "That kiss downstairs—so out of character for you in too many ways to count—tells me you're terrified of him."

She shifted on her feet but couldn't look away because of

how he held her. "I just didn't expect to see him. Now that I know, I'll be ready. I'll be fine."

He scowled. "There's that word again. Fine isn't good enough."

Castor released her, stalked to the wet bar, and got out strong whiskey. If she didn't know him better, she would say he was furious. No. That idea was ridiculous. Castor in a rage brought lightning, and none was coming. Not even static electricity.

"Are you afraid of him?" He poured a couple of fingers in two glasses, picked them up, and crossed the room to her.

She took the glass he offered, took a sip, and made a face as the sharp taste of alcohol hit her tongue. "There's nothing Kaios can take away from me now. And with my own personal superhero around as a bodyguard, he can't hurt me." She tipped back the rest, coughing at the sensation of the fumes burning the hairs out of her nose.

"I'm hardly a superhero." He muttered the words before he tossed back his own.

She wondered if he was thinking of his wife's demise. Leia had never learned the details beyond that he'd had a wife who was gone. But, as a demigod, did he blame himself? Or had she been human, and he'd had to watch her go?

Either situation was heartbreaking. Still, he was *Leia's* hero. If his heart for the people he helped hadn't won her over, the way he tried to protect her now would've sealed the deal. Not that she'd ever tell him. Even if he had kissed her back, he wouldn't want it. She was his assistant only.

Instead she waved a hand. "I can handle a werewolf." Maybe. "Besides, demigod trumps werewolf every time."

He choked out a rare, rusty-sounding laugh. "Don't let them hear you say that."

She dredged up a smile and handed him her glass. "I think I'll take a nice long bath if you don't mind."

As she turned away, he called her name. She looked over her shoulder, eyebrows raised in question. "I won't let him hurt you tomorrow, Lyleia."

The unmistakable sincerity in his voice was almost her undoing. "Thanks," she managed around the lump taking up permanent residence in her throat. She made her escape to the bathroom with more haste than grace. Whiskey was her kryptonite, and as the kiss Castor laid on her downstairs combined with the affection in his gaze just now, she was fighting the urge to wrap her body around his. If she could get through the next few days without making a total idiot of herself—or dying—maybe she'd rethink the direction her life should take after this.

Whatever that was.

Chapter Eight

Castor waved away the waiter who'd wheeled in a cart of food with a gruff "thanks" and fiddled with the placement of what he'd ordered, setting the items up on the coffee table before moving the cart out of the way.

Stupid to feel edgy. He was the son of Zeus, a successful and very rich man with a mostly fulfilling life. And he was about to make a romantic gesture.

Nerves strung tight through him, making him as edgy as a nymph at one of Dionysus's orgies.

Leia had been in that bath for ages. Damn tempting to join her but making a move on her tonight would be the worst possible timing. Yes that kiss had given him hope—until she'd stated it was a ruse at least—but with everything she was dealing with, all because of him, only an asshole would try something.

This was about Leia.

She'd looked so fragile, her pale skin practically translucent, only emphasizing dark circles under her eyes, as she'd gone into the bathroom. Trying so hard to be brave, but werewolves were fucking unpredictable and dangerous because of it, and this one clearly had it in for her.

To have to face him…

Castor shook his head and tweaked one of the dishes into a better position. He hoped. Aesthetics for an airplane were more his thing than arranging a relaxing meal.

"What's this?"

He turned and his nerves settled at the sight of her. Dry, wrapped in a white terry cloth bathrobe, something black and silky peeking out the bottom, and damn appealing, her blond hair a cloud around her face.

"How do you do that?" he asked.

Now he was turning into her with the non sequiturs.

"Do what?"

"Come out dry and…perfect." He couldn't stop his voice from dropping on the last word.

Her cheeks turned red, which only made her more appealing, but she also smiled. "It's a nymph thing. Part of our…magic…I guess you could say."

"Handy."

"Very."

He shifted. "This is for you."

Her eyebrows went up, but curiosity had her coming closer to inspect what he had. After a second, she bit her lip. "You got me all things to hydrate?"

He shrugged. "Yes."

"That's just…" She shook her head as she trailed off.

Just what? Adorable? Creepy? Concerning? Not part of their relationship as boss and employee? What was she thinking? He honestly couldn't tell. "Sit down."

At her small smile, he realized that he'd basically barked an order. But he felt foolish enough at this point, no way was he taking it back.

Besides. She sat. "Herbal tea. A cucumber salad. Coconut

water. Several kinds of juice. And noodle soup." Again with the small smile. "You've thought of everything."

He eyed the assemblage of items. "It's what I could get on short notice. I guess it is a bit of an odd mix."

"It's lovely."

Two words guaranteed to make him feel like more than a demigod in her eyes. "I thought about starting the fire but wasn't sure if that went with the theme or would counteract the hydrating."

"Actually, a fire would be nice," she said, sitting down. She poured herself some of the herbal tea and sat back, wiggling her bare feet up onto the couch with a sigh.

He picked up the remote and clicked a button. "Modern humans have taken away displays of manliness," he commented.

That got a full laugh from her. By Olympus, he loved that sound. Clear and sweet, like bells, or the gurgle of a brook.

"You should laugh more," he said, before he could stop himself.

Leia sobered. "I haven't had much reason to."

"I get that." He glanced at the seating. He knew what he should do. He should take the armchair and give her space. This was about taking a moment for her.

He just couldn't quite make himself do it. Instead he grabbed her by the ankles and lifted, gently so she didn't spill her tea, and sat down with her feet across his lap. "Do you have a thing with feet?"

She frowned over her cup. "With feet?"

He shrugged. "Some people don't like their feet touched."

She lowered the cup to look at him sideways. "I guess that depends, Castor. What are you planning to do to my feet?"

"Nothing weird." He leaned over to pick up a tube marked "soothing gel." "They told me at the spa that this was...great." Actually, the lady's word was orgasmic, but he wasn't saying that. Tonight wasn't a seduction, dammit.

"Oh." Leia blinked. "That sounds nice, but I tell you what. How about you do my feet and I'll do yours."

"No thanks."

"I feel bad being the only one getting the full treatment here." She waved at the goodies. "It's only fair."

"I'd rather not."

Leia studied him with narrowed eyes. "*You* don't like people touching your feet. Do you?"

"Do you want the goo, or not?" He shook the tube at her.

Shoulders shaking in silent laughter, she nodded. "Please."

Luckily, her feet were already clean and bare, her toes neatly trimmed and painted a soft pink. Castor squished some of the gel into his palm, smoothed it over the bottom of her foot and, trying to be gentle, worked it into the skin, giving her a foot massage at the same time.

"Oh, wow." Her moan went straight to his dick.

This was a bad fucking idea. He should've got her the hydrating things and left the room, because now all he wanted to do was make her moan again.

"Has anyone ever told you you have magic hands?"

Castor opened his mouth to answer, only her hand shot up. "If you say something like only in the bedroom, I might kick you," she said.

He huffed a tight laugh. "Actually, I was going to say that my wife liked foot rubs."

The words left his mouth and he waited again for that sharp lance of pain, but none came. Just a pleasant warmth with the memory.

Meanwhile, Leia looked at him with a hundred questions in her eyes. And Castor found himself wanting to share this part of himself that only his brother knew.

"Pollux and I captured our wives and stole them from

our cousins, who they were promised to. Hilaera was a priestess of Artemis, and we'd grown up together. Hers was an arranged marriage and he did not love her."

"But you did?" Leia asked softly.

Castor nodded. "Since we'd been children. I was young and stupid and arrogant as most demigods can be. It's hard to be taught humility when you have the strength of the gods running through your veins and are surrounded by puny humans who adore you. The things Pollux and I did to our mother…" He shook his head.

"I can just picture it. That poor, poor woman."

He snorted a laugh. "Don't you believe it. She was a juggernaut and we loved her the most until the day she died."

The curse of immortality and loving humans.

"Anyway, Hilaera and I ran and had one spectacular year together and she became pregnant with my child. But the goddess Artemis—my half sister by technicalities—was angry that I'd taken one of her priestesses and told my cousin where to find us. I was out hunting when he attacked."

Castor broke off and closed his eyes, concentrating on the motions of his hands as he worked on her feet. "She and my unborn child were both burned to death in our home."

"I'm so sorry," Leia said softly.

Many had said the words before, but somehow with her they struck true, like Eros's arrows, and the pain of the memory that had coiled around his heart like a hydra, squeezing the joy and life from his life for ages, melted away.

Was it possible for a demigod to find happiness? Most of his bastard cousins, spawned by various gods, had only found misery.

Still, immortality meant that with time all things were possible.

"Me too," he said.

"If you did things like this for her, she was a lucky

woman." Leia wiggled her feet. "Heck, if you did this for me regularly, I might sell you my soul."

She was trying to lighten things up for him. After watching her with the employees they helped through his secret giving, he knew her generous heart hated to see anything in pain. It didn't mean she cared for him, just that he was in pain and she wanted to help.

But Castor sent up a prayer to his father, something he hadn't done in a thousand years. *If she gifted me her heart, I would cherish it. Always.*

Chapter Nine

Castor stood at the front of the chapel beside Marrok, who appeared as cool as ever while he waited for his bride. Not being a love match, and more of a business deal, that was probably about right. Except they were going to have to go through the mating tonight. Wolf shifters had strange traditions.

Like the exterior, built in natural stone, the interior of the building was simple, constructed of thick pine logs. Pews carved from matching wood stood in rows with a single aisle down the center, a deep red velvet carpet leading up to the altar and pulpit. Floor-to-ceiling windows at the front revealed an incredible view of the lake, which glittered under the brilliant light of the full moon.

Kaios was already seated in the front row. Marrok had pointed the werewolf out when he'd come in, commenting that he and Tala had been shocked when the man had shown up unannounced.

"We invited them, of course. All our ancestors are invited. But werewolves don't usually bother with wolf-shifter matings," Marrok had said. "It must be because we're both alphas."

Castor had murmured something vague and hoped to Hades that was the case, though the better scenario was for the werewolf to move on before he caught sight of Lyleia.

Marrok suddenly gave a low whistle.

"What?"

"Did you see Leia before coming here?"

"Yes."

"Was she dressed for the wedding yet?"

"No." She'd preferred to come to the ceremony without him, a decision that had bothered him more than it should. She'd muttered something about needing to sit near the back. Whatever that meant. Best guess, she was avoiding the werewolf who'd ruined her identity as a nymph. The only thing keeping him from ripping out the bastard's neck when they'd been introduced ten minutes earlier was not wanting to ruin his friend's important day. That, and Leia had warned him not to before he'd left the hotel.

Dark laughter lurked in Marrok's voice. "Let's just say you're going to need a very large stick."

Stick? What the fuck was Marrok talking about? "Why?"

"To beat off the wolves."

His friend was obviously enjoying the hilarity of the situation but had to be mistaken. Leia was gorgeous, but she didn't flaunt her beauty, tending to dress on the conservative side. Besides, he doubted she wanted to call attention to herself with Kaios here.

He scanned the crowds filing in at the back of the chapel. "I don't see her."

"Navy dress. Her hair is up."

Navy sounded right. Conservative. The way his nymph liked to dress.

He caught a flash of blue and the top of her golden blond

hair piled high on her head. Then the tuxedoed man blocking most of her from view stepped aside. What was Marrok talking about? While she looked incredible to him—his body started to heat up and harden at the sight of her like it always did—he harbored feelings for her. Given the way the other ladies were dressed, he doubted Leia had anything to worry about with the wolves.

The dress was long, draping to the floor, the top gathered over her right shoulder. No cleavage showed. A thin slit at her hip showed a sliver of flat belly. Sexy as all Hades. But still covered up compared to the skin on display from the lady wolves. Leia appeared classy in a room full of overdone.

She caught his eye and waved. Her lips, painted bright pink, stretched wide in a smile. Castor caught his breath as his stomach clenched in response. Her smile was for him alone. How he knew, he wasn't entirely sure. His heart hadn't tripped over itself like this since he'd captured his wife. Only this was different, not stronger exactly, but...different. Hilaera had been familiar, his love tender. With Leia he was all fire and need and protectiveness. Leia pointed at the back pew, indicating where she intended to sit.

Someone he couldn't see snagged her attention, though she seemed reluctant to turn away from him, but she did.

Castor inhaled sharply.

The back to the dress was...there was no damn back to the dress. The garment was held in place by a thin strap or two across her shoulders and dipped low to a point above her curvy derriere. Barely above.

"Holy hell." His body, already charged by the intimate smile she'd graced him with, responded rapidly. He shifted his stance, trying to ease his discomfort. In the meantime, every man around her did a double take. What was she thinking?

His friend had the temerity to chuckle. "You're a lucky man."

"She's my assistant."

"Right."

Yeah. He didn't believe it, either. Not with how much he wanted her—a desire that went way beyond the physical. Her humor, her prickliness, her intelligence, her vulnerable strength all combined to make her the woman she was. A woman he craved with a fierce need that seemed to wrap around him now.

Unable to leave the front where he stood with Marrok, Castor kept a close eye on Kaios, in case the werewolf discovered Leia's presence and decided to make trouble. Meanwhile, he gritted his teeth as, one after another, men introduced themselves to Leia.

Mine. He had the strangest urge to hurl the claim at them, but she wasn't his. Yet. Besides, he didn't behave like an uncouth youth. Ever. This woman was driving him out-of-his-mind crazy.

Leia politely conversed with each potential suitor, sending them away in short order. Eventually she sat, her gaze seeking him again. He chuckled when she rolled her eyes, his own tension easing a smidge. Those other men stood zero chance.

Twenty minutes later, the double doors to the church opened to admit the bride. Beside him, Marrok stilled as the entire church hushed.

Tala was radiant in a form-fitting dress that hugged her lithe body to her knees where it flared out. She'd left her chin-length dark blond hair down, her veil framing her lovely face. Every man in the place had to reel their tongues back in.

"*You're* the lucky man," Castor murmured.

"I hope so."

Castor didn't comment, too busy observing Leia.

Rather than watch the bride, she'd turned, he guessed to see Marrok's reaction. Her expression softened, and her gaze slipped to him. Finding Castor staring at her, she yanked her gaze back to Tala, a soft blush coloring her cheeks.

Satisfaction tore through him. Leia wasn't indifferent. She couldn't be.

Every nuance of that kiss slammed into him. He'd put all thoughts of it away, thinking it had been a gimmick. A ploy for her to avoid Kaios like she'd said. But had it been only that?

As Tala neared the front of the chapel, Leia's gaze once again moved to him, skittered away, returned and stayed. Her blue eyes drew him, like the moon holding the ocean in its sway.

He held his breath, fighting every instinct to go to her and drag her out of there.

With a reluctance that bordered on out of control, he shifted to face the front of the chapel, breaking the searing moment of intimacy when he'd rather it go on and on. Thankfully, the ceremony was over in short order—the wedding portion of wolf-shifter matings tended to be brief as everyone wanted to get to the next part. The tension would escalate more and more until they completed their actual mating. The buzz of it filled the room, sending a charge through his system.

Turning again, he sought out Leia, only to find she'd disappeared. Unable to go after her, he kept his expression neutral, searching discreetly for a flash of navy silk or of blond hair. Someone, a woman he assumed, pinched his butt as he followed Marrok and Tala down the aisle. He didn't bother to discover who. It wasn't Leia.

She'd never be so crass. Even if he wanted her to.

Yearning and anticipation hung heavy in the air as the gathering made their way out of the chapel, along the river, and over a wooden bridge that led them into the woods. The pheromones were flying. Heady stuff. As their lives were linked in the church, in the mating ceremony, so too were their bodies.

The pull of the alphas, the lust, dragged on Castor, but he forced the sensation to the back of his mind, his attention squarely on finding Leia. Perhaps she was afraid of stirring up the nymphs again or getting into it with her nemesis and ruining the mating? A quick check showed him Kaios was still with the group. She couldn't be in danger off by herself.

Castor might need saving, however, having already refused three women and peeled one off his right side to plaster her against another man more appreciative of her attentions. He'd already passed one couple who couldn't wait, going at each other around the side of the chapel. As the group walked, more and more peeled away. The sounds of moans and grunts and heavy breathing started to join those of the breeze and the river.

Once deep in the woods, the wedding guests still with them stopped, allowing the bride and groom to continue on into the trees alone, to a secret spot Marrok would have prepared ahead of time. There they would mate in private... though rumor had it some couples didn't wait to be secluded before having their fun.

As the guests stood, the need ramped higher. By now he was hard as a rock, heavy and aching in a way he'd never experienced before. More couples paired up and wandered off, unable to resist the need to claim each other that the mating ceremony stirred in their bodies. Not everyone gave into temptation, but many did.

"Are you here with someone?"

Castor glanced down at a brunette who'd been poured into her slinky red dress. "Yes. Sorry."

She gave him a disappointed pout. "I don't see anyone here."

"She gets nervous around nature. Don't worry, we'll make up for it later."

She sighed, managing to squeeze her breasts together at the same time, which did nothing for him. "Nature isn't a thing to fear. It's a thing to revel in." She trailed a hand down his arm.

He plucked her hand away. "I'll be reveling with my date."

She tossed her hair. "My loss. If you change your mind…"

He wouldn't be changing his mind. Only one woman would satisfy him.

A strange rushing noise, similar to the sound of ocean waves, pulled his attention to the river off to his left and Castor froze. Every cell clicked into his power in gut reaction as a wall of water burst up from the bed of the river below.

"What the—" someone exclaimed behind him.

The forest exploded into disarray around them. All of the guests dropped to the ground as the wind whipped the trees into a frenzy. Pine needles rained down, filling the air with their zesty scent. Birds screeched their protest as they abandoned their nests and perches. One of the largest trees groaned a horrible protest as it appeared to uproot, only to be righted by a blast of water.

Several of the guests around him screamed, but none of the chaos approached them, as though they were cocooned in a bubble of protection. Castor's jaw dropped at the awesome display.

This had to be all the nymphs. Whipping around he searched for her among the chaos. She wasn't with the guests. Where the hell was she?

Then he found her.

Lyleia. His nymph stood on dry ground at the bottom of the lake near the chapel, though the water didn't touch her, pushed outward from her body by an invisible force. He doubted anyone else could see her. Although wolves had excellent vision at night, demigods had better, and he'd been searching for her. Somehow, he knew he'd always find her wherever she was.

Eyes glowing an eerie blue, arms raised above her head, she pushed the wall of water higher. A cool mist brushed his face and dampened the fine cloth of his tux.

He knew exactly what she was doing, especially after the little display from the nymphs in the area when they'd been here talking to Calli before. Leia was making a big damn point. Not an attack against her brethren, per se. More a display of her hurt and anger.

He didn't know how he knew that, but he did.

His nymph was smart. If her family wouldn't help her, she'd force their wrath, which would, in turn, result in a display of nature run amok. Because in demonstrating, she was whipping up the other nymphs, forcing them to use their powers against her, manifest a "sign from the gods" for Tala and Marrok.

Fear gouged a hole in his chest. Surrounding Leia on all sides were ten or twelve nymphs who were clearly furious, if their scowls and glowing eyes were anything to go by.

"Lyleia." He barely breathed the word, but she turned her head in his direction, as though called. He started toward her, compelled to help, but halted when she shook her head. Her pale hair swirled around her face, whipped by the winds assailing her.

Nymphs of various kinds—water, air, fire, earth, electricity—raised their hands. In another explosion of sound and shock waves, they pummeled her with the elements they controlled.

Except none of their efforts touched her.

In fact, she pushed away everything they aimed at her, redirecting it over the forest. How she held them off while controlling the water at the same time, he had no idea. She was magnificent in her effortless use of her power.

Did anyone else suspect? Or was her ploy working?

Where the fuck was Kaios?

A glance around him showed none of the other guests had discovered her. All were too focused on the forest going wild around them. Kaios was across the field from where Castor stood, which meant the wall of water should block Leia from the werewolf's view. But Kaios stood strangely still with an expression akin to fury tightening his features, his lips drawn back in a sneer.

Castor split his attention between Leia and Kaios, but the man stayed where he was.

The culmination of the mating was nearing—instinct screamed at him as pressure seemed to build all around them. Pressure that had nothing to do with Leia's actions, and everything to do with the mating magic.

The urge to relieve the need pulsing through him grew to an unbearable ache. His hand went to his cock, gripping through the fine cloth of his tux, tugging. It wasn't enough. He needed to bury himself in the sweet softness of a woman. For hours. His body told him only Leia could assuage the desire riding him hard. Her display of power had him even more turned on. His fear for her safety, and his demigod instinct to protect her, heightened his need even more.

He wanted to rescue her and sweep her away from this place to their own private mating.

Would she even let him touch her? By the gods, he hoped she would.

A burst of desire pummeled through him, like the wave of water Leia wielded. Groans arose through the gathering of wolf shifters and a handful of other magical creatures in attendance, shouts echoing through the woods as couples reached their own completion in turn.

In the same instant, the cacophony of noise from the forest and river ceased. The water splashed back down to the bedrock with an almighty roar. Stark silence settled over the woods.

Marrok and Tala must have completed the mating.

"A sign." The cry started with one man. "The gods have spoken. They've blessed this union." Quickly the phrase caught on, repeated in hushed whispers by the rest of those who'd witnessed the storm of nature.

For his part Castor inspected the now calm lake with troubled eyes. Where was Lyleia?

Chapter Ten

A hush fell over the crowd as Tala and Marrok appeared. Then, as if an unseen signal had been given, all the wolves bowed to the alpha pair. After a pause, they both lowered their heads in return to the assemblage, then walked through the group to lead them all back to their cars. The celebration was set to be held back at the hotel.

Tension coiled in Castor's shoulders, tightening the muscles until they strained against his bones. Leia still hadn't shown up, but he had to act as though nothing were wrong or all her efforts would be for nothing. He followed the bride and groom and got into the limo with them along with Tala's maid of honor, her sister Astra.

Other than flushed faces, Tala and Marrok appeared well put together given what they'd just been up to. The couple sat close together on the back bench seat, with Castor and Astra taking opposite side seats.

"Was that Leia?" Tala asked as they pulled away from the parking lot, breaking the awkward silence which had descended.

"Yes." Worry had the one word grinding from him.

"Where is she?" Marrok asked.

"I don't know. She disappeared under a wall of water." And he couldn't do a fucking thing about it.

"We should go back." Marrok reached for the button to lower the window between them and the driver, but Castor shook his head.

"She's a water nymph," he said. "She can handle it. Besides, she'd be upset if we ruined her work by giving away the secret to everyone. She'll be fine." She'd promised him she would, and he'd made sure Kaios had left with the crowds.

You'd better be fine, he thought. If she wasn't, he'd wring her neck for taking that kind of risk.

The rest of the interminable ride was completed in silence. Castor shifted his position a few times. While the worst of the pheromones were released with the mating, being near the couple was still like a constant bombardment of lust, like standing chest deep in ocean waves. Marrok couldn't stop touching Tala—not overtly, just constant contact. All Castor could picture was Leia's big blue eyes, her hair fanned out on a pillow like a golden halo as he moved above her, the sound of her husky voice groaning her pleasure.

Where was she?

The valet handed them out onto a red velvet carpet. A woman with deep red hair approached with a come-hither light in her eyes. "Congratulations, Alpha. You as well, Alpha." She nodded to Tala and Marrok in turn. Then she hooked her arm through his. "And who might you be, handsome?"

"Mine."

Relief and lust warred for dominance at the sound of Leia's warm voice behind him. He shrugged off the redhead and turned, the impact of just seeing her like running chest first into a gorgon's fist. He pulled his nymph in close where he could wrap his arms around her and feel for himself that she was unharmed and inhaled her rainy-day scent.

"I can take a hint." The other woman's parting comment hardly penetrated.

He was too busy with the woman in his arms, bending his head close to murmur in her ear. "I didn't see you after the ceremony."

Wolves had phenomenal hearing, which meant he couldn't ask her straight out if she was okay. A question like that would sound odd to anyone who overheard.

"I made it safe and sound."

She did appear to be unharmed. In fact, she looked perfect, her hair back up as it had been at the wedding, not a drop of water in sight anywhere on her person. Unable to resist the urge, he leaned forward and planted a light kiss on her unsuspecting lips. He wanted to linger, sample, taste, and take. However, now wasn't the time. Not yet at least.

Her eyes widened, but she didn't protest.

He grinned, relief and triumph raising his spirits like a balloon in strong wind. Question and answer time could come later. After she faced the werewolf who'd destroyed her life.

Castor sobered. Be damned if that werewolf would ever harm her again. He offered her his arm. "Shall we beard the lion?"

Her lips quirked, but she accepted the gesture, hooking her hand through. "By all means."

Forcing his body to calm—at least he wasn't the only man walking around in discomfort—he led her into the hotel.

Off to the right the sounds of a lively gathering drew them through a set of double doors into a ballroom with windows all along one wall and the original bar along the other. A dance floor took up one end, and the rest of the room was dotted with large, round tables set with fancy linens and china. Large bouquets of flowers graced each table, filling the room with the sweet fragrance of spring, helping to mask the natural outdoorsy scent put off by the large gathering of wolf shifters.

Castor searched the room for Kaios, tensing against the werewolf's presence, but didn't see him among those gathered. Leia found their table while he was detained by one of the elders from Marrok's pack. As he watched, she circled the table, fiddling with something by the plates. Then she dropped off her purse in a chair and rejoined him.

Before he could ask her what she'd been doing, the newly mated couple was announced. Then everyone found their assigned places for the sit-down dinner.

"My, my, my," a rough male voice intoned from behind them. "I thought that was you earlier, Lyleia."

She didn't so much as twitch, but her sudden tension radiated to Castor nonetheless. The demigod in him wanted to wrap himself around her and shoot lightning bolts through the man, but he understood this was Leia's fight. Holding back with effort, he reached under the table to take her hand, which was clenched in her lap. Her fingers loosened up to link with his. She plastered a fake smile on her lips, one Castor recognized from when she'd first started working with him, and turned to face her tormentor.

"Kaios."

No doubt even the wolf shifters starting to join them at the table picked up on the tension radiating from her. It pulsed like a living thing.

"How lovely to see you after all this time." The werewolf actually had the audacity to lean in for a kiss.

"Touch me and I'll stab you with my fork." Leia delivered the threat with her polite smile in place and a friendly tone to her voice.

Pride swelled along with his dick. Damn, she was

amazing.

For his part, Kaios froze, took a moment to assess how serious she was, and apparently concluded she meant it. Castor had zero doubt she did. He kind of wished Kaios would try something, just to see Leia fork him somewhere that would cause permanent damage. Weren't werewolf balls a delicacy in some societies?

"I took the liberty of moving your seat as far away from mine as possible." Leia glanced meaningfully across the table.

Castor choked back a laugh. So that's what she'd been doing earlier. He and Kaios, as the most powerful beings present—even if the werewolf was an unexpected addition—were both treated as guests of honor, seated with the bride and groom, but that didn't mean Leia had to sit close to the man.

"Out of respect for Tala and Marrok, I won't share our story with them," Leia continued.

Kaios's lips flattened then pulled back in a silent snarl that had Castor's fists bunching. Werewolves were notorious for hair-trigger tempers and a tendency toward crazy.

Visibly schooling his features to amusement, Kaios stepped back. "I would have thought you'd learned from the last time." He tut-tutted. "Still high and mighty. Even without your spring, hmm?" He made his way around the large round table to the opposite side.

Castor's entire body tensed with the need to lunge for the man's neck. Leia's only reaction was to tighten her hand around his, holding him back. Rage burned a cruel path through Castor's chest—at Kaios as well as at himself. He shouldn't have let her do this.

"She's not alone anymore," he said, biting off the words.

Deliberately, provocatively, Castor trailed a finger across the smooth skin of her upper back and placed a proprietary hand at her nape. Claiming.

She turned her head to blink at him, a question in her eyes. He returned her gaze with a warm smile, solely for her. One he meant. Satisfaction zoomed through him as she shivered beneath his touch and her eyes darkened to the hue of a midnight ocean. He'd started this for their audience of one, but Leia's shiver had him laser focused entirely her. With wicked intent he trailed his fingertips down her spine in a feather-light touch designed to tease. At the same time, he dropped his gaze to her strawberry-colored lips, eager for another taste.

"I see. Found yourself a new lover, Lyleia?"

But beyond a scowl at the use of her full name—*his* name for her—Castor kept his gaze locked with Leia's. He swallowed at the need he could see in the color in her cheeks, the sparkle in her eyes.

"Castor is a wonderful man. I'm lucky to know him."

Suddenly, with everything inside him, Castor wished she meant it. That she did think him wonderful. That she felt lucky because she was his.

He gave himself a mental shake. "I should thank Brimstone."

"You know Delilah?" Tala asked, clearly happy for a different topic.

He nodded. "She found Lyleia for me."

"She's fantastic."

"She must be a fantastic pimp," Kaios said with a sneer.

Castor leveled a hard glare on the werewolf. "Watch it."

"Or what, demigod?" the werewolf spat.

Castor sent an enigmatic smile across the table and had the satisfaction of seeing the werewolf pause. Between the two of them, he'd know Castor was more powerful.

The waiter appeared and set down a steak in front of the wolf. Castor flicked a hand and lightning shot from his fingertip, zagging across the table and hitting Kaios's plate. A small thunderclap followed, making everyone in the room jump. The tang of burnt ozone mixed with the smoky scent of charred meat. What had been a rare piece of meat was now black and crispy.

Leia turned her head into Castor's shoulder, trying to hide her laugh in the silence that followed his small demonstration of power.

Usually he let people guess his parentage, letting what they didn't know worry them. Even more rarely did he whip out his control of lightning in a blatant display, but Kaios was too full of his own power and importance. The guy needed knocking down a peg. He might have bent Poseidon's ear, but Castor's father was Zeus, and the king of the gods trumped his oceanic sibling.

And now Kaios knew that Castor could turn a bigger wrath on him.

In fact, that sounded like a damn good plan.

Kaios had realized the implications if his glare, even as he pinched his lips closed, was anything to go by.

Castor picked up his knife and fork, cut a small piece from his own steak, which was still a lovely pink, and offered the morsel to Leia. She shook her head at his actions, the amusement dancing in her eyes. Amusement and gratitude. She opened those lush lips over the bite then gave a delicate groan of delight that stoked the tension inside him, like coal to a steam engine.

"Delicious," she murmured.

Unable to resist any longer, he leaned forward to kiss her lips. "Delicious is right."

An adorable blush stole up her cheeks. He wanted to take her back to their bedroom and find out if her entire body blushed the same way.

Marrok cleared his throat. "And I thought *we* were

throwing off pheromones tonight. I think you two are giving us a run for our money."

They both laughed at the alpha's attempt to break the tension, though Castor could tell Leia's giggle was forced. He didn't miss the flash of hatred in Kaios's eyes. Disguised quickly, the burn was unmistakable. Pure, unadulterated hatred.

Castor scooted closer to her, needing to protect. What had Leia done to him?

Dinner over, at Tala's sister and maid of honor Astra's prompting, Tala and Marrok stood and moved to the center of the room.

Castor knew his role as best man. A tradition at alpha mating ceremonies was for the alpha to put on a display of his skills. He gave Leia's hand a squeeze and reluctantly left the table to retrieve Marrok's weapon of choice for his display. As maid of honor, Astra also got up to get Tala's for her.

Tala and Marrok laughed when they discovered they'd each chosen throwing knives. Duties done, Castor returned to his seat. The alpha pair put on an impressive showing, culminating in both throwing a knife at the other as they stood still against opposite walls.

"Wow," Leia whispered when it was over. "They're very evenly matched, but in different ways. Good thing they mated rather than battled for the right to be alpha."

Castor agreed.

Following their display, the bride and groom shared their first dance, after which the floor was open to everyone. And it was needed, because the sexual tension had built back up in the room with the physical displays.

Needing to get her away from the werewolf—and also closer to himself—Castor pushed his chair back, stood, and held out a hand to his date. "Dance with me?"

She stayed where she was and pursed her lips. "Maybe

that's not a good idea."

"What? Don't dance?"

"And if I said I didn't?"

"I'd say you can put your feet on top of mine."

She shook her head, biting down on her smile.

"Come on," he urged.

"I'll pass."

He leaned down and placed his lips close to her ear. "I *want* to dance with you."

Still she hesitated.

"Please?" He found himself holding his breath like this was the first woman he'd ever asked to dance. If Pollux could see him now, his brother wouldn't let him live it down.

When he'd about decided to give up and sit back down, she placed her hand in his and got gracefully to her feet. "Just remember whose idea this was."

Not hers. He got the message.

He led her out onto the floor. The DJ was still playing slower songs as people wrapped up eating. He pulled her into his arms, and his hand at her waist encountered bare skin, warm and silky under his fingertips.

"I can't believe you did that," she whispered. "Lightning? Really?"

"No one threatens you around me."

She shook her head, but he could see a warmth in her eyes that hadn't been there before.

"Every man in this room hasn't been able to take his eyes off you tonight in this dress."

She chuckled softly. "The same way every woman hasn't been able to stop stripping that elegant tux off your body with their eyes. We're all driven by the same urges tonight, and they don't come from us. They come from them." She tipped her head at Tala and Marrok, currently circling the room together greeting guests.

He was tempted to challenge that idea, knowing this thing between them had started before coming to Colorado. At least for him. Knowing Leia, she'd pull away if he did, and he wanted her close. Besides, he could hardly argue with his erection pulsing and the pressure inside him needing release.

She stepped on his foot.

"Ouch."

"Sorry."

"Was that in retaliation for saying you're beautiful?"

Another clash of feet, only this time she managed to plant the spiked heel of her stiletto on his instep. "Sorry," she muttered again. "I did warn you."

She pulled a disgruntled face. He chuckled at how cute her consternation was, only to receive a glare. He sobered. "Yes, you did."

Despite his clamoring body, he kept the rest of their dance PG, managing to get stepped on only a couple more times, and escorted her off the floor when the song ended, feet sore and body on fire. Thankfully, Kaios had moved away, talking to wolf shifters on the other side of the room. Though Castor continued to watch him closely.

They spent the rest of the evening together, except when Marrok needed Castor for various best man duties. At those times, Castor made sure he left Leia with Tala's sister or one of Marrok's many cousins, the female ones at least, determined to never leave her vulnerable.

Several hours later, even though the party showed no signs of winding down, Leia tugged on his sleeve. "I'm dead on my feet."

He'd hoped the connection that had been forged between them would lead to greater intimacy in their room, but she did appear to be drooping and pale. Had using her powers in such force today wiped her out? He swallowed back his disappointment even as his protectiveness where she was concerned kicked in hard. "Have Astra walk you up. I won't be too much longer."

He watched as she threaded through the crowds to wish Marrok and Tala goodnight before she disappeared out the side door with Tala's sister.

"She's quite a woman."

Castor glanced over to find Kaios standing beside him. Rather than bothering to answer, he went to move away.

"Did she tell you about how we met?"

Castor ignored the question. "If you value your life, you'll stay the hell away from me."

"It was a ceremony similar to this one only for werewolves. The effect of a wolf mating can be amazingly heady. Don't you agree? Imagine it when the mating pair are more... powerful creatures." The werewolf's implication was blatant.

A lie. Leia had already told him how things went down. But had she held back? Not told him everything? Something to explain the werewolf's hatred.

Suddenly picturing Kaios possessing Leia's body as the sexual tension drove them to greater heights had Castor wanting to punch a hole through the arrogant smirk on the werewolf's face.

Instead, he forced himself to turn and walk away.

Chapter Eleven

Something pulled Leia out of the dreamless comfort of slumber. Instinct niggling at her, she blinked awake then stilled to discover Castor perched on the edge of the bed.

She glanced at the clock. Two a.m. She rubbed her eyes as she sat up to face him, dragging the heavy blanket with her to cover her black silk nightgown.

She did her best to ignore her instant awareness at his nearness, trying to tell herself it was unspent sexual need from tonight. Not real. And not something he'd want acted on. Only, turning off her own needs had no effect. "Castor? Is something wrong?"

At some point during the evening, he'd discarded his tux jacket and tie and rolled back his sleeves. Yummy. He blew out a breath and ran his hand through his mussed hair. She frowned at the outward sign that her usually cool-headed demigod wasn't at all calm. "Sorry." He paused and shook his head. "Sorry," he said again. "I'll go."

She put a hand on his arm, stopping him. "What's wrong?"

"I had an interesting conversation."

She took a moment to think through that. "Did Kaios get to you? Please tell me you didn't get in a fight or anything." She searched for any signs.

If anything, his eyes turned darker, more penetrating, like he could see into her soul. "I showed an impressive amount of restraint. You'd be proud."

Ah. She drew her knees up to her chest and wrapped her arms around them. "Did he imply we slept together?"

He shrugged. "I didn't believe him."

"No, but wanted to punch him I'll bet. Which is probably what he was hoping for. What an ass." Was Castor jealous?

"Yes. He is."

He watched her with an intensity that wrapped around her like a spell being cast.

"I humiliated him," she said in a low voice.

Castor said nothing. Just waited.

And it all came spilling out. Half drowning the damn werewolf in front of men he'd wanted to impress. The werewolf mating ceremony had been held near her spring. They'd all been gathered. Rare then. Even more rare now.

"It was such a stupid thing to do," she muttered at the end. "Werewolves are unpredictable, and that's on their own." She shrugged.

"So he came after you."

Another shrug.

Castor put a hand under her chin to tip her gaze to his. "I'll never let him touch you again."

Leia lowered her gaze, hiding her thoughts, wishing that could happen, but knowing she'd have to leave after this ceremony, disappear like she had before. Especially now that Kaios knew of her relationship with Castor—or thought he did anyway. Needing a distraction, she took his hand and flipped it over, tracing the lines of his life across the palm.

"According to this you're going to have a long and prosperous life."

"Lyleia." There was a growl to his voice that told her he was on edge more than she'd realized.

She lifted her head to peek at him only to be snared by the look in his eyes.

Wanting. Real wanting, and not for show.

An ache of need glowed low in her belly. Could he tell the effect he had on her? Here, in the dark room, after the things that had happened, she couldn't resist the pull he had on her anymore. Didn't want to.

He flipped his hand over to lace their fingers together, tugging her toward him. "You thought I'd be just like him when you first came to work for me?"

"Did you know about my history when I came?" she asked, stalling.

He shook his head. "Only that you no longer had your spring. Is that what you thought?"

"Yes."

"Do you still think that?"

He drew lazy circles on the inside of her wrist with his thumb—a soft caress that befuddled her mind. "No."

"When I first told you about the mating, was your past experience your only reason for refusing?"

She licked her lips. "No."

His gaze turned sharp, searching. "What else?"

The heat in his eyes scorched her skin everywhere they trailed, or maybe her visceral response to this man was the culprit. Either way, the truth was dragged from her lips. "This."

He tipped his head in question, clearly wanting clarification. Time to take a risk. She hadn't used her sexual radar in centuries beyond shutting direct approaches down or turning her own needs off. She hoped to Aphrodite the skill wasn't rusty, that she was reading his signals right.

Never taking her gaze from his, she slid out from under the blanket and climbed into his lap, straddling him. No mistaking the evidence of his desire. With excruciating slowness, she lowered her lips to hover above his, not quite touching. "This."

She didn't have to wait long. With a low groan he covered her lips with his, his tongue sliding along hers, tangling and tempting. He tasted of champagne and something delicious that was simply Castor. He tangled his hands in her hair to angle her mouth better and shuddered as she opened fully for him, whimpers of need pouring from her into him.

Leia lost herself to his kiss, his touch, her body taking over from her mind as she surrendered to the sensations that she'd felt building since the first moment they'd met. This thing between them went way beyond the desire brought on by a wolf-shifter mating. This weekend had only exposed a nerve. Something she had a suspicion they'd *both* tried to ignore.

She whimpered and rocked against him. Not enough skin. With frantic fingers she reached for the buttons of his shirt, but he placed a hand over hers, stilling her actions.

"Are you sure?" The raw need in his voice almost had her coming right there.

Still, she gave the question the consideration it deserved, taking a deep breath. "Yes." With her free hand, she smoothed the fine material of his tux shirt over the toned muscles of his chest, savoring the heat of his skin beneath. He shuddered at the touch.

I shouldn't be doing this.

She needed to resign when they got back to Austin. Not only because of the danger Kaios presented, but because allowing herself to fall for Castor had broken all the rules.

But she couldn't make herself stop. "I'll no longer be able

to work for you, but for now..."

She raised her gaze to his to see an answering need reflected back at her.

"I'll take 'for now,' but promise me you won't make any decisions about later without discussing it with me first."

Why did that request leave her spinning? He wanted what? More? To keep her as his assistant after slaking his lust? Even knowing she'd let her desires get the better of their contract? If she was honest, in this moment, she didn't care.

He released her hand and she undid the buttons on his shirt. Not in a rush like earlier, but one at a time, teasing him with light brushes of her fingertips with each inch of exposed skin. His breath quickened with every touch. Finally, she peeled the shirt off him. With a grin she leaned forward and gave him a playful nip on his pec, at the same time releasing a wave of pleasure through them both, a perk of being a nymph.

"Holy shit," he muttered, his cock throbbing between them.

In an instant, urgency took over and together they caught fire. Holding her in his arms, he stood, then lowered her feet to the floor.

He gazed down at her body, encased in the tiny black negligee. "Damn, honey. You're killing me."

She giggled even as she delivered a smile worthy of all nymphs. The rest of their clothes were divested in a rush, with heated kisses between every move, every delicious sweep of their hands over each other.

Leia squealed as he spun them around and tumbled her back to the bed. He followed her down and she wrapped her legs around his back. Hovering above her like this, his hot skin was a brand against her own, claiming her with the contact alone.

And everything, all of it, felt so right.

With incredible gentleness, he smoothed her hair back

from her face. "I've been waiting for this so long, I don't want to rush."

Her eyes widened. "So long?"

He nodded. "Since that time we worked together on the Huntington contract late into the night. You were helpful, smart, and challenging."

She raised her eyebrows. "So you lusted after my brains and sarcasm?"

He grinned and brushed a thumb lightly over her nipple, pulling a gasp from her lips. "Yes. Plus, you touched me."

She smoothed her fingers over the dark stubble on his jaw. "I've touched you before."

He leaned into her caress. "Yes, but that was the first time. Before then, you held yourself back. Noticeably careful to keep your distance. But you lost that reserve for a second, and it was...electric."

She remembered. "I thought it was just me. Or the fact that you're the son of Zeus."

He shook his head. Then he lowered his head and took one rosy peak of her breast into his mouth. Warmth and heat and the rasp of his tongue assaulted her senses. She groaned and tangled her hands in his thick hair, holding him to her. He grunted as another wave of her power pulsed through them. The more she let go with him, the less she could control it.

After giving attention to each breast, he proceeded to explore her body in a leisurely drive-her-to-the-edge kind of way. No part of her went untouched as he built the tension in her body to screaming pitch. She adored how every caress was like he worshipped her body. Finally, when she was on the point of begging, he made his way back up to her lips. He captured her in a drugging kiss as he ran a hand up the inside of her thigh where he slipped a single finger inside her.

He groaned low and pulled back to grin down at her. "So ready for me."

"Mmhmm," she agreed, distracted by what he was doing with that hand now.

He rolled on a condom, and she had no idea where it came from. Didn't care. Then he positioned himself at her entrance. "So damn sexy."

"You're not the only one who's been thinking about this." They both gasped as he eased inside her, pleasure throbbing, escalating.

"How long?" he demanded, every inch a demigod.

She tossed her head back as he started to move, rocking her hips into his, matching his rhythm.

He stopped moving. "How long, Lyleia?"

She opened her eyes to find him hovering above her, an intensity in his gaze she'd never seen before, even as passion tightened his features. "Too bloody long."

He grinned, and she sighed as he started to move again. She closed her eyes, reveling in her body and his and their joining as sensation layered on sensation.

"Eyes on me." His rough demand had her obeying to find him watching her with an intensity that only built the pleasure.

Gazes locked, with each stroke inside her, and each shudder of pleasure, the pressure built and the wonder became personal. As though he was branding her as his own. Electricity skated over her skin.

As her eyes widened, he smiled. Triumphant and arrogant and hers. "You're not the only one with pleasurable tricks."

"You haven't seen anything yet." With an answering triumphant smile, she let loose the fullness of her gift and the pleasure inside her rose like the swell of a tsunami, so intense she dug her nails into Castor's back, hanging on for the ride.

Castor groaned, thickening inside her, and increased his pace, bucking into her wildly, his face beautifully harsh above hers.

The electric charge gathered and sparked in his eyes then shot between them, sizzling lightning wrapping his cock in electric pleasure that flirted with pain and made each thrust that much more intense.

Leia writhed beneath her lover, wild with pleasure as their powers entwined until, with twin shouts of rapture, they toppled over the edge into another world, one filled with exquisite sensation. He didn't stop his thrusts until both of them were satiated, drained.

Leia relished the slowing after the beauty of what they'd created together, the weight of his body delicious as they lay locked in replete contentment. She refused to think about the later. The consequences and next steps. Not yet. She still wanted now too much and worrying about later tended to ruin now.

Castor buried his face in her neck, then hummed in appreciation. "You smell like rain and mountain springs... and me."

She opened her eyes to find him watching her with a lazy, satisfied, utterly possessive smile playing across his lips.

"Gods, you are an incredible woman. The most beautiful thing I've ever seen."

"I find that hard to believe given how long you've lived but thank you." She stretched, luxuriating in the way his gaze followed every curve of her body, showing off like the nymph she was, accessing a part of her she hadn't in way too long.

He captured her face between his hands, suddenly all serious intent. "I mean it, Lyleia."

She turned her head to kiss his palm. "I believe you."

He nodded, satisfied. Then stood and scooped her into his arms.

"What are you doing?" Even as she asked the question, she wrapped her arms around his neck, happy to go anywhere he wanted to take her.

"I'm making us a bath. I've heard a man hasn't lived until he's made love to a water nymph in the water."

The rumors were true as water amplified the effect of their pleasure giving and receiving ability, partly why gods pursued them as relentlessly as they once had. The experience became addictive. Panic surged through her. She laid her palm over his heart. "I don't do that."

He paused and looked down at her. "With anyone?"

She shook her head.

"Ever?"

She glanced away. "I guess you could say I'm saving it for my forever, not just one night of passion."

A single finger under her chin tipped her gaze back his way. "I won't say I don't want it, but I get it."

"You do?" She'd expected the ego she knew lurked behind that easygoing exterior to rear its head.

"I had what I thought was forever once. For an entire year. So yeah, I do." He went from seriously sweet to heart-stoppingly intense in a nanosecond as he gave her a wicked grin. "Besides, I have lots of other fantasies where you're concerned."

"I may have a few of my own," she murmured, body humming.

"Like what?"

She toyed with the hair at the nape of his neck. "Like… can demigods really go all night long?"

She sent out a pulse of wicked pleasure and grinned as the result became obvious against her hip.

Dimples flashed as he grinned back. He was doing that more and more. Smiling.

"Let's find out, shall we?" he asked.

Leia squealed as he spun fast, showing a small hint of the extra strength and speed demigods often inherited.

Chapter Twelve

She needed to recharge her system.

With that sole need in mind, she tossed back the covers and tried to stand up, only to be stopped by an arm curling around her waist and dragging her back into bed.

"Where do you think you're going?" Castor nuzzled her neck.

She laughed. "You're insatiable, and I need a shower."

He didn't let her up. "I wasn't the only insatiable one."

She giggled, then sobered, teasingly serious. "I don't know what you're talking about."

He grunted his amusement as she peeled his arm from her. Not bothering to cover up, she padded across the room naked.

"I could get used to that sight in the mornings."

She didn't respond to his mumbled comment, pretending not to hear. Reality wasn't something she was ready to face yet, and those words came under the heading of *later*.

Once she was in the bathroom, she decided a shower wasn't going to cut it. She needed water immersion. With a flick, she turned the knobs for the oversize spa. Once the tub was filled, she lowered herself in and leaned back, closing her eyes with a sigh, and letting the magical properties of the water seep into her skin. In an instant she was transported in her mind. Rather than bathwater, the pristine water of a warm spring surrounded her, the air fresh and clean.

"What have you done?"

The whispered words were barely audible. Leia sat up with a jerk, sloshing the water over the side of the tub. "Calliadne?"

But her sister wasn't anywhere to be seen.

Must be more tired than I thought. She lay back in the water.

"What have you done to us, Leia?"

Her eyes flashed open. This time the voice was unmistakable. Calli was trying to talk to her.

Leia sank beneath the water and waited. "I'm here, sister."

A shimmering version of Calli's face swam before her eyes, iridescent and rippling with the water. "You've brought destruction on your own people."

Leia shook her head. "I knew what I did last night wouldn't make you happy, but I did it for the right reasons."

"Your actions have brought death upon us."

Leia gripped the sides of the tub hard. She hadn't hurt anyone last night. Stirred them up and pissed them off, sure. "What are you talking about?"

"Kaios. When you first lost your spring, he warned us to stay away. Now he's brought a warlock."

Why? Why attack the nymphs? "But you had no part in it. I made you react to me." Calli's image wavered and faded. Seconds later, pain exploded through Leia, like a shard of ice being stabbed into her brain and down her spine. She curled in on herself and screamed in agony, the sound gurgling out into the water still clear as day to her nymph's ears. She knew this pain. It could mean only one thing. One of her brethren was dead.

Arms plunged into the water and scooped her out. "Leia?" Castor's frantic voice penetrated the haze of pain.

She pried open her eyes. "My people are under attack," she gasped out.

"What are you talking about?"

Through sheer will, she swallowed down the acrid taste of bile and forced the pain from her body. A couple deep breaths and the agony wasn't gone but pushed back. "Put me down."

He stood her up, and she ran to the bedroom and started pulling on clothes—whatever was at the top of her suitcase, which happened to be jeans and a black T-shirt.

He followed. "What are you doing? What's going on?"

"Kaios is attacking the nymphs by the chapel in the woods. He has a warlock. I have to help them."

Castor didn't ask more questions. Instead he started pulling on his own jeans and T-shirt.

"What are you doing?" she asked.

"Coming with you."

"No—"

"Demigod." He pointed at his chest. "And your..." She held her breath for whatever else he thought he was to her. "Boss," he finally said. "I'm coming with you."

She didn't argue. In silence they finished dressing, she pulled her hair back in a quick and messy ponytail, and they rushed from the room. Castor pulled out his cell phone. "Marrok. We have a problem."

He quickly explained the situation to the wolf alpha, then hung up and put his phone in his pocket. "They'll be right behind us. With help."

"No help."

"Why?"

"If their people find out the sign from the gods was a lie, it will ruin everything."

"You sure?"

No. But the last time she had tangled with Kaios she had lost everything, and everyone, dearest to her. She didn't want to risk the two alphas. "Yes."

He pulled out the phone and handed it to her as they reached the car. "You call them. I'll meet you there."

She frowned even as she reached for the phone. "How—?"

"I'm a lot faster than any car." Right. Demigod.

She dialed as she got in the car and strapped in. Marrok picked up immediately and she told him the same thing she'd just told Castor.

"I'm still coming," Marrok insisted. A female voice sounded from another room. "So is Tala."

"Okay. But no one else."

"Agreed."

She hung up and headed into war.

Chapter Thirteen

"Kaios!" Castor bellowed.

He had made it to the chapel, which appeared peaceful except for the dry-as-a-bone lake and riverbed. Finding no one there, he'd made his way down the path and across the bridge, into the forest. There chaos reigned, and the scent of ill-used magic hung heavy in the air.

He bellowed Kaios's name again.

No answer amidst the harshness of screams and shrieks. At the side of the river, he found Calli curled into a ball with her hands clasped over her ears. Blood was oozing from her eyes, ears, and nose.

He grasped her by the shoulders, and she flinched, but otherwise didn't respond. "Where is he?"

She couldn't answer. The rasp of her lungs told him she might be inhaling blood as well.

"Calli? No!" Leia appeared at his side. He didn't ask how she'd found him.

"What's wrong with her?"

"She needs water." She pulled a bottle from her backpack.

He hadn't even realized she had it with her. She poured half the bottle over Calli's face, then tipped it to her lips. The nymph gulped it down as fast as she could. The bleeding stopped and her breathing improved.

"How'd you know?"

She glanced at him. "It happened to me when I lost my spring. Nymphs are used to being in their element most of the time."

"And yet, you manage."

"I've gotten used to going without for long periods. I take lots of baths and carry water everywhere."

"Help the others," Calli choked.

"Is there any water left?"

Calli shook her head.

Leia turned to Castor, her face pale and pinched with fear. "I can't help you."

"What if I can get you water?"

Hope speared through Leia at his words. "Can you do that?"

Every protective instinct hammered him to fix this now. "Son of Zeus. Remember?"

She searched his face and he knew exactly what she was thinking. If he could bring down rain…

"Do it."

Castor stood, his feet planted wide, his hands balled into fists at his side. Leia visibly shivered as a cold wind whipped through the trees. The previously fluffy white clouds above gathered, forming a massive thunderhead that grew black and heavy with rain.

Castor raised his hands, and lightning illuminated the sky. In a rush of sound, a deluge descended on them, and in seconds they were soaked to the skin.

In Leia's arms, Calliadne sucked in a grateful breath and sat forward.

"We have to fight," Leia told her. Her sister nodded.

Together they stood and clasped hands.

"Keep it coming," she called to Castor. He didn't break his concentration to acknowledge her words, just kept the rain coming, drawing it forth.

As he watched, Leia and Calli manipulated and directed the water. Raindrops banded together to coalesce into first a pool at their feet, then a raging river, and finally a wall of solid water.

"Hold on to something," Leia warned Castor. He wrapped his arms around the trunk of a massive tree, his fingers digging in as though the thing were made of butter instead of hard pine.

Together, the two nymphs sent the wall of water crashing through the trees, taking out everything in its path. Nature in full force could be a real bitch. So could a pissed-off nymph or two.

With a roar to rival a tornado, the torrent slammed up against the mountainside as far as a mile away, frothing up the granite walls only to turn back on itself.

Castor held on, still clinging to the deeply rooted tree, until the water receded. He spat out a wad of leaves and pine needles. "Did you get him?"

Leia shut her eyes and seemed to listen, her brows drawn low, mouth tight with concentration.

She gasped, her eyes springing open. "No. He's going after the Hyleoroi, forcing them out of hiding."

She crumpled in on herself as though she could feel her brethren's pain. Hyleoroi, the nymphs who were watchers of the wood, started screaming.

"Castor!" Leia screeched.

Fury took a back seat to physical pain, like razors over his skin at the sight of his nymph in such distress, electricity building inside him to toxic levels.

He had to fix this. Now.

And there was only one way he knew how. With determination, Castor settled, closed his eyes, blocking out Leia's moans, and waited. He'd learned to detect the feel of power being used around him, like a tickle at the back of his neck, just as Zeus had taught him after claiming him. Searching for power in use was a trick he'd never fully mastered, but he'd try anything now to help Leia. If a warlock was involved, he'd leave a signature.

There. In his mind's eye, he could see a bubble at the center of the woods. A murky gray color, it pulsed with each spell the mage cast.

"Stay here."

In a flash Castor sprinted to the location. The speed with which he could move made him almost invisible to the naked eye. To him, the forest flew past in a blur of greens and browns with patches of white snow still at the base of some trees. Before the wizard knew he was there, Castor slammed into him. With the might of his strength, he threw the man into the side of the mountain, knocking him out cold.

The screams hushed and silence settled over the area like a thick blanket had been placed over them, muffling any noise. Not a creature dared move or even breathe in the wake of the madness.

Then a bird's cry pierced the air and life returned to the forest, almost as if every living thing around him sighed with relief.

Tempted to toast the guy with a bolt of lightning, Castor slung the warlock over his shoulder, sack-of-potatoes style, and ran back to where he'd left Leia and Calli. Their eyes still glowed bright blue, the way Leia's had the night before at the mating ceremony when she'd used her powers—the sight both eerie and sexy as sin.

"Is that the mage?" Calli asked as she washed away any

remaining blood in the river, which now flowed peacefully. Only pieces of limbs floating by gave any indication of the horrors wrought only moments ago.

The trees still dripped with water from the earlier dousing, sounding like a sprinkle of rain, and the ground squelched beneath his boots. He was glad he'd brought clothes other than his nice suits, although he hadn't anticipated needing them for this reason.

"Yes," he answered the nymph.

"Where's Kaios?" Leia asked.

"No sign of him."

"Damn." She turned to her sister, taking Calli's hands in hers. "I'll make him pay, if it's the last thing I do."

Calli's lips flattened. "We *all* will. No one's attacked us like that before. He's more dangerous than we realized."

A grim sort of anger thundered through him. "I see. So you'll let him ruin one sister's life, but not all of you?" Castor couldn't hold in the bitter question. The unfairness of how they'd treated Leia, shunning her, had his blood pounding in his ears with impotent wrath.

Leia, for her part, shook her head at him. He dumped the mage on the ground, uncaring of how he fell, and crossed his arms—unrepentant.

"You're right."

He raised his eyebrows at Calli's words. "Of course I am."

Leia rolled her eyes. "That's enough out of you, Superman. Let's not worry about the past." She faced Calli. "Can you get the word out to everyone? I'm worried he'll try something else."

"I'll talk to them."

"As a werewolf, our ancestor and here because of our mating, he's our responsibility." Marrok and Tala appeared in the clearing. Tala sported a baseball-size bruise on the side of her face.

"What happened?" Castor asked.

"We ran into Kaios in the parking lot." Tala touched the welt and winced. "There's a reason he's stayed alive this long. We couldn't stop him."

Damn their luck. "Why not?"

Tala glared at Marrok. "Because someone was too busy trying to protect a woman who didn't need protecting."

Marrok said nothing. His jaw working wasn't a good sign, though.

"So…what next?" Leia asked.

Castor made a split decision. "We call Delilah."

"Good idea," Leia agreed. "She takes care of all manner of supernatural issues. I'm sure she'll have an idea. And I'm sure she could arrange additional protection for the nymphs here, in case he comes back."

"I think you're right," Tala said. "She's a resource we can use." She turned to Marrok. "We might want to make a call to the Alliance before we have dragon shifters involved."

Her new mate nodded. "Agreed."

"In the meantime, let's tie this mage up and gag him. Calli?"

The nymph glowered at the unconscious man on the ground. "We'll hold him here until you come for him. Arrange protection for Leia, as well."

"Why?"

"He's hated her for a long time."

Marrok's eyebrows winged high. "He didn't come for the mating ceremony?"

Leia shrugged. "Who knows? Maybe he doesn't like the idea of two alphas mating. It'd give your packs too much combined power. He's not a rational man."

Guilt weighed heavily on Castor's shoulders. He had put Leia in this position. He'd brought Kaios's wrath down upon her by bringing her here with him and getting her mixed up in this. If he'd left her in Austin, none of this would have happened.

"I think he'd already found me," Leia said.

Castor snapped his gaze to her. "What?"

She gave him a look he couldn't interpret. Regret maybe? "I don't have proof, but I think someone broke into my apartment. Twice. In the last month. I was...going to resign."

That's why she was going to resign. "I saw the letter."

She blinked. "You did?"

He nodded. "And now that I know the reason for it, like hell I'm letting you go."

Leia opened her mouth only to close it. "Let's talk about it later. We should go."

Regardless of how they'd gotten in this situation, he'd be damned if that werewolf got anywhere near her this time. Castor waited while Leia gave her sister a hug and whispered something in her ear. Something that sounded like, "I'm so sorry."

He hated that she felt she had to apologize. If her sisters had supported her to begin with, Kaios wouldn't have been the threat he was. Biting down on harsh words, he placed his hand at the small of her back—he needed to touch her, reassure himself she'd come through this okay—and walked back to their cars with her, Marrok, and Tala.

"You're soaked." Leia made the observation when they were about halfway back to the hotel.

He grinned. "I'll tell anyone who bothers to ask that you dunked me in a river."

She chuckled. "I guess it has an element of truth. Why did I do that?"

"Because I needed a cold shower?"

That surprised a laugh out of her. The husky timbre of it went straight to his groin. How he could be turned on after what they'd just dealt with, he had no idea. She drove him to reactions that weren't normal. "It won't be far from the truth."

She turned wide eyes on him, then glanced at his lap. Her lips parted in an adorable *O* of realization. "But it was only supposed to be one night."

Not if he had anything to say about it.

Chapter Fourteen

The ring of her cell phone dragged Leia out of a deep sleep—
one induced by multiple bouts of sex and orgasms. She still
couldn't wrap her mind around the situation, but she was still
going with it.

After attending a business meeting for Castor to negotiate
pricing on a private plane for the new combined pack, and
then going to a mating event that evening—a barbeque held
in Rocky Mountain National Park where the pheromones
returned to whip the attendees into a frenzy—they'd returned
to the hotel and spent most of the night wrapped in each
other. Pleasure upon pleasure. And in between, he'd held
her, unable to stop touching, as they talked. About nothing.
About everything.

Somehow, they'd managed to get to the plane. Leia had
sat in her usual spot, a different row than Castor, only to
have him get up and move to the seat beside hers. He hadn't
said anything, merely given her a reproving look. Then he'd
proceeded to whisper dirty words in her ear about exactly
what he wanted to do to her body but refused to touch her.

As punishments went, it had been torturous. By the end of the flight, she'd been squirming in her need and her panties soaked.

He'd taken them back to his house. The second they were inside, he'd put into action every one of those intentions.

She'd been to his house before, even inside his bedroom. She liked it. Unlike the modern furnishing in his offices and many of his planes, Castor had decorated his house more traditionally—lots of dark woods and masculine colors. In particular, she loved his king-sized bed with its massive wooden four-poster frame.

With a groan, she leaned over the side of the bed and fished around in her purse for her phone. "Hello." Her voice came out as a sleepy rasp. She cleared her throat.

"Leia, it's Delilah."

"Oh. Hi, Delilah." She glanced over at Castor, who stiffened beside her. They had yet to hear anything about Kaios or the warlock. "What can I do for you?"

"Is this a bad time? I wanted to discuss what to do with the warlock. I should have him in hand shortly."

Leia glanced at the clock and winced. Of course, Delilah would expect them to be in the office now. She sat up and the dark blue satiny sheet fell into her lap. Castor's gaze tracked the sheet, then lingered, firing her blood. But she needed to concentrate, so she gathered it up to cover her naked breasts. "I'm running a little behind today."

Castor tugged at the sheet. She made a face and shook her head at him. He laughed silently back at her but released it. "Um. Tala and Marrok should be included in the discussion. Let me call you from the office? Say an hour from now?"

"That's fine."

Leia hung up and dropped the phone back in her purse. "We need to get going."

Before she could roll off the bed, he moved with that

crazy speed again and had her pinned beneath him, sheets gone, and evidence of his not-yet-waning desire obvious between them. "Nope."

"We're already late." Her protest was weak, even to her ears, as a familiar need fizzed through her veins, setting her nerves alight.

He smoothed his hand down her side from breast to hip to thigh. With a tug, he wrapped her leg around his waist. She shuddered as he repeated the action on the other side.

Then, with one slow stroke, he entered her. Leia tossed her head back, arching to take him deeper.

"Eyes on me." The demand was one she'd heard frequently from him this weekend. Castor wanted to watch her face, her expression, as he brought her to the pinnacle of pleasure and over into the abyss. The intimacy of making love while staring deeply into his eyes, and he into hers, snagged at her heart every time, filling her with love until she was bursting with it. Though she'd managed to keep that to herself.

He took his time now, each move deliberately slow. She could feel every inch of him, and the pleasure built inside her.

"Please…" she begged.

"Please what?" His low tone, darkened with need, made her shiver.

"I need you."

"You have me." He plunged in deep.

Her stomach contracted at his words. She did have him. For now. She wouldn't let herself wish for—

"*More*." She groaned the word as the tingling warning of her impending orgasm started in her middle and spread outward.

"You have all of me."

Those words sent her tumbling into dark pleasure. Wave after wave surged through her and she cried out her fulfillment. She couldn't pull her gaze away from the intensity in his. A declaration of love trembled on her lips. Instead she pulled him closer and pressed her lips to his, pouring her emotions into the kiss.

You have all of me. Seductive words. He meant those words. By the gods she wished he'd meant them the way she wanted.

. . .

Afterward, they managed to shower and dress quickly. Luckily, she'd packed extra clothes for their trip. She donned a dark brown pantsuit with matching jacket, one of her favorites because of the wide belt and oversize buttons which gave the jacket a certain flare. Castor, always immaculate for work, emerged from his closet looking especially fine in a gray suit with subtle pin striping, a matching vest, and a deep red tie.

Unable to help herself, she crossed the room and fiddled with the tie, getting it just right. Lifting her gaze, she encountered tender affection in his which about stopped her heart.

Leia gave a satisfied nod. "Better." She stepped back, giving herself space. "I need to get my car. Can you drop me off?"

Before the trip, he'd picked her up and taken them both to the airport. He cocked his head. "I'll drive us both to the office."

"I'd rather drive myself."

He narrowed his eyes. "Why?"

Was there annoyance in his voice? "This thing between us is private. Showing up at the office together is not exactly the best way to keep it that way."

His lips flattened. "Are you embarrassed to be with me?"

Demigods and their pride. "Absolutely not. However, we

are still employer and employee." She waved a hand between them. "At least in the office. Let's enjoy this privately for a while before complicating things. Okay?"

And in case he tired of her quickly. She'd rather keep that to herself. Although she couldn't reconcile a cold, calculated love-her-and-leave-her with the man she knew Castor to be. But, in her experience, sex changed all the rules. Changed people.

What if it *had* just been the pheromones?

Her adamant denial that she wasn't embarrassed must've mollified him, because he stopped scowling. He wasn't happy either, but he also didn't push it. "Okay. I think I get it."

After grabbing her car, they both headed into the office, where they first called Tala and Marrok, then got Delilah on the phone.

"You have all of us on speaker," Leia told her.

"There's been a development since I called earlier."

Leia's heart dropped into her stomach and rattled around in the hollowed-out emptiness there.

Castor trailed a hand down her arm, the action soothing, but she couldn't help glancing at the glass wall of the conference room. No one was walking by, but they could have been.

"What kind of development?" he asked.

"The warlock is dead."

"What?" The question shot out of her before she could say it in a calm, rational manner.

"I guess the Covens Syndicate didn't want to anger the gods. They sent Greyson Masters, their best hunter, after him."

"I guess that takes care of that." Marrok's dry tone came across loud and clear over the speaker.

"Before he died, we did get some information from him. Based on his comments, it sounds as though Kaios's appearance had two purposes. He'd discovered Leia was alive and has been stalking her for some time. In addition, it sounds as though the werewolves truly are concerned about Tala and Marrok's mating."

Marrok's voice came over the speaker. "But werewolves are outside the Federation of Packs. What do they care?"

"My guess is there's concern because your mating gives you too much power within the wolf-shifter community," Delilah said. "Creating the biggest individual pack within the Federation. I should've seen that coming when I suggested it to you."

Castor, leaning fisted hands on the conference table, shook his head. "He used that as an excuse to get close to Leia."

Made sense. Leia closed her eyes briefly. If the werewolf had manipulated Poseidon, he'd do the same to his own people to get what he wanted. Her dead, it seemed.

"But why go after the nymphs?" Leia asked as she opened her eyes.

Delilah spoke. "According to the warlock, Kaios wasn't sure of Leia's involvement at the ceremony. He needed proof to take back to the werewolves. Though more to get permission to kill Leia from what we could gather."

"He didn't have a clear view of Leia from where he was standing," Castor said. "I doubt he was sure of her involvement until he got it out of the nymphs when he attacked them."

And Kaios thought of her as pathetic and powerless after he took her spring, so likely didn't suspect her capable of what she'd done.

"The nymphs refused to tell him," Delilah said.

"They refused?" Leia asked, voice choked.

"Yes," Delilah confirmed. "That's why he set the warlock on them...to force their cooperation."

Her sisters had stood up for her? Before she'd helped save

them, and after what she'd done to them? Why?

"Is Kaios after us, too?" Tala asked.

"At least to discredit you for the lie," Delilah said. "Though I'd say in a peripheral way."

"Any sign of him?" Tala asked.

"Not yet, but I have my feelers out," Delilah said.

"We should all be careful until he's found," Marrok advised.

There wasn't much more to discuss. As they hung up, Leia sank back in her seat. "Kaios had the warlock killed. He used the coven." Anything to make it difficult to trace back to him. He'd done that with her spring, manipulating a god to enact his own revenge.

"What?" Castor knelt down in front of her, hands on her knees, familiar in a way they'd never been in the office before now. And she soaked it up. "Why would you say that?"

"I know that werewolf and his sick mind. We can't prove Kaios was there that night, but the warlock could have. He's tying up loose ends."

"Hopefully he'll go back down a hole to wherever he came from and stay there."

She ran her gaze over her demigod's face, every adored plane. Those amazing eyes looking back at her with tender worry, those kissable lips that could both master and persuade flattened with an emotion she couldn't quite identify. If she hadn't known better, she would have said love. Her heart fluttered, but she ruthlessly squashed the hope. Being the object of his attention was like being caught in gravity, orbiting around him.

Only the tension in his hands gave away the fact that he was way more tense than he wanted her to believe.

He's going to go after him.

Dread wrapped icy hands around her neck, squeezing hard, choking her. Castor was a demigod, programmed to go after monsters. And this particular monster had come after his lover.

Shit.

Why hadn't she seen this earlier? Castor wasn't going to risk Kaios coming after her again, and Kaios wasn't going to quit popping up like evil whack-a-mole. Double down on things getting worse, Kaios saw Castor as a block to getting at her now.

Gods, how could she have been so stupid? Kaios would come after Castor next.

Time to disappear. Again. Only this time, she was forcing that werewolf to face her directly. She wouldn't let Castor risk his life. Not for her. If he died…

Bile seared her throat.

She pasted a calm smile on her face, the one she'd used with him countless times over the last year. "I'm sure you're right. He won't risk poking his head up right now."

He remained silent, searching her gaze for any hint of her feelings, but she'd mastered keeping people out when she wanted and regarded him with serene patience. Finally, he gave a nod. "Good girl."

She rose to her feet. "I have emails to get through."

"Yes." He stood, too.

She could feel the burn of his gaze as he watched her leave the room and close the door behind her.

She did exactly as she'd said, letting the daily routine of work take over. She went through emails, made calls, and skimmed through a presentation the marketing department wanted to present to Castor next week.

At noon Castor opened the connecting door. "I have a lunch meeting," he reminded her. She waved him out of the room and even waited an extra ten minutes in case he came back for any reason. When she was confident he was gone, she picked up the phone and dialed.

"Delilah. I need to disappear."

"I was wondering when I'd hear from you." Her friend didn't sound surprised at all. Of course, Delilah had been the one to help her pick up the pieces and move on with her life last time. "What does Castor think?"

"He doesn't know."

"I think you should discuss it with him. He's a demigod. He can protect you."

"And add him to Kaios's crosshairs." The werewolf had shown, in her brief experience with him, that he didn't fight fair, and he held a grudge. Gut instinct told her he wasn't done.

Silence greeted her declaration.

Leia winced. Delilah's only directive when she'd placed her in this job was not to fall in love with her boss.

"Like, that is it?" No sensor filled the other woman's voice.

Leia winced again. She'd let Delilah down. "I'm afraid so."

"How does Castor feel?"

"He's in lust. And I enjoyed what time I could get with him."

"I don't blame you. Love, the real kind, not just lust that burns itself out in time, doesn't happen as often as humans wish."

"No, it doesn't."

"You're sure it's only lust for him?"

"Yes."

"Okay. Let me work on a plan. I'll get back to you later today."

"Thanks, Delilah."

"I only want you to be happy, Leia."

Leia closed her eyes. Happy didn't tend to be a goal of hers, but Delilah had been a true friend to her. "I owe you."

"No, you don't."

Chapter Fifteen

Castor watched Leia work without alerting her to his presence. Sometimes being both fast and silent was helpful, such as when he wanted to sneak up on his assistant. He leaned in the doorway, arms crossed, and smiled at the look of utter concentration on her face. The gods had made an angel when they designed her. His heart squeezed at the mere sight. No woman had ever affected him this way.

A tiny shard of guilt pricked him at the realization that even Hilaera hadn't caused this urgent need—not only to possess, but to protect, to cherish, and to care for—within him. He was like a teenager again, only more than he'd ever been during the short years of his youth before he'd basically stopped aging. The tiny tip of her pink tongue peeked between those berry-ripe lips. He wanted to see those lips parted in passion. He adored how she lost control with him when she was in total control at all other times. A stirring of desire had him shifting position, which caught her attention.

Her head came up. "Oh! I didn't hear you."

He smiled. "Sorry."

She gave a mock glower. "Sneaky man."

Once upon a time, she'd have used a meaner term than man. He took that as a good sign. Sleeping with him was a huge step, but that could just be physical attraction. They worked well together, and she'd admitted to having feelings for him. But feelings didn't mean love, and she was acting strangely today. More...distant.

"Any plans tonight?"

He asked the question as casually as he could. Her only reaction was a quick check of the time. If she was about to do what he suspected, his nymph was phenomenal at hiding her true emotions.

Before she could lie to his face, he continued. "I'm playing poker with Pollux and some friends."

"Oh." She turned those cobalt eyes his way. Guileless eyes. Maybe he was wrong.

"I think it would be a good idea for you to stay at my place tonight, though."

She frowned. "Why?"

"With Kaios still on the loose, I don't like the idea of you on your own. What if he attacks you?"

"Did you know more than fifty percent of personal attacks happen in the home?"

"Lyleia—"

She waved a careless hand. "I doubt that's going to happen. He has to be wondering what personal protection I have in place now."

She didn't need anything but him. "It's not worth the risk."

Leia's lips flattened in a stubborn look he recognized. "I'm not staying with you, Castor."

His heart dropped to his feet at the blatant rejection. Only his suspicion of what she was up to kept him from going all demigod and claiming her here and now. "Why?"

She was silent a beat. "I'd think it obvious."

"Not to me."

"Don't be so dense then."

"I am never dense," he growled. He needed her to think she had him fooled.

She ground her teeth. "You are the most frustrating man."

"But you kinda like me for it."

She gave a little snort. "To be clear, our relationship went from boss/employee to lovers recently. Given things are in a…transitional phase, living together, even short term for my protection, is a bad idea."

"Transitional phase, huh?" He didn't like that. He didn't like any of this. Especially that he had no idea of her true feelings for him—whether this was lust and a quick fuck, or something more.

She gave him a look that dared him to continue with that train of thought.

He held up his hands and sobered. "Okay, not staying at my place. At least have Delilah arrange protection at your apartment or a different place to stay."

She pursed her lips.

He moved into the room and leaned his fisted hands on her desk, staring her down. "This is non-negotiable, Leia. If you don't, I'll camp out at your door."

She gave a little huff. "Fine. I'll talk to Delilah."

Castor gave a satisfied nod. "Have Delilah's protection detail meet you here."

She narrowed her eyes at the command.

"How about dinner at my place tomorrow night?" he asked before she could argue.

Rather than answer, she searched his face. "You want to continue with this?" She waved a hand between them. "Whatever is between us?"

Continue? He wanted forever. He just wasn't sure if telling her would scare her off. "Given you woke up in my bed this morning—"

With a quick glance she checked the door behind him. "You didn't just say that in the middle of my office," she muttered.

"*You* called us lovers," he pointed out. "Yes. I want to continue. Do you?" He held his breath and waited for her answer.

She stared at him, as if debating.

Come on, honey, be honest with me. Let me in.

"Dinner tomorrow sounds...wonderful. Can I bring anything?"

He released his pent-up breath in a silent whoosh. "That sexy black thing you had on the other night wouldn't go amiss."

"Seriously?" She held her hands wide, indicating the office. "Still at work."

Castor chuckled and gave her an unrepentant grin. Even worried about her, he felt lighter than he had in centuries. "So, tomorrow night?"

"It's a date."

He pretended not to notice how the answering sparkle in her eyes had dimmed. He wasn't wrong about what she was really planning. "Excellent. See you then." With a wave he strode out of the office, only to turn around at the elevator and stride back into their office suite.

"Forget something?" she asked.

"Yes." He came around the desk and bent to take her face in his hands. "This." He laid his lips over hers in an urgent kiss filled with all the emotion this extraordinary woman provoked in him.

Someday, she would learn to trust him with her whole heart. Until then, he'd do everything in his power to make sure she stayed and was safe.

He pulled back, savoring the womanly taste of her, to gaze into her startled eyes. "To remember me by."

She cocked her head, lips twitching. "I wasn't likely to forget."

For her sass, he planted another kiss on that delectable mouth. "Bye."

"Bye." He liked the husky note that had entered her voice. She definitely wasn't physically averse to him. The question was, where was he in her heart?

As he waited for the elevator to bring him down to the parking garage, he mulled over his next steps. If Leia had her way, he wouldn't see her tomorrow. She'd done a magnificent acting job trying to convince him all would continue. However, after their call with Delilah this morning, for a brief flash he'd caught the look of tenderness she'd cast his way. His heart had tripped over itself in the hope that perhaps her feelings ran deeper than simple lust. But he'd also seen the flash of panic immediately following.

She was going to do a runner. He was certain of it.

He was equally certain losing her was not an option.

He didn't have to wait long before Leia appeared in the parking lot. Alone. Did the woman have zero common sense? Staying far behind, he followed her home to her apartment. She lived in a new complex in downtown Austin that boasted shops on the first level, like living above a shopping center or outdoor mall. Her apartment, the one or two times he'd been in it, was tastefully decorated exactly how you'd expect a nymph's taste to be—all blues and water themes, a large freshwater fish tank taking up one entire wall of her living room. He'd found it tranquil.

He discarded his jacket, leaving it in the car, and rolled up the sleeves of his white dress shirt. He gave her enough time to get deep into packing before he headed upstairs to catch her.

He knocked at her door. "Leia?"

Silence.

"I know you're in there. Let me in." He knocked harder.

Silence.

"Leia? I won't force my way in, but I'm not leaving until Delilah's protection shows up."

More silence.

She hadn't left. He would've seen her go.

Castor pounded on the door now. "Leia?"

No answer.

He checked that no one was watching and gave the door the tiniest kick. It burst open, splintering the wooden doorframe where the lock was. A quick search of her apartment showed him Leia was gone. Castor pulled out his phone and dialed the only person he could think of.

"Where is she?" he demanded.

"She's protected," Delilah answered.

He had to concentrate on not crushing the phone. "Protecting her is *my* job. Tell me where she went."

"Funny, she sees protecting *you* as *her* job."

He shook his head. "What's that supposed to mean?"

"It means she loves you. How you managed to get her to feel something other than numb is a miracle."

Leia loved him. His stomach clenched with elation and roiling fear for her safety. "Delilah...if anything happens to her and I'm not there, I'll never forgive myself."

Chapter Sixteen

Leia's gaze roamed over the wooded scene beyond the window over the kitchen sink. As places to hide went, this one was idyllic. The napaeae wood nymph who dwelled here had been nothing but welcoming. A nice change.

After she had given Castor the slip, she'd met up with Delilah, who'd flown her back to Colorado. There, Tala and Marrok had stepped in and hidden her away in a tiny cabin, one that smelled of the pine trees the logs had been hewn from, in the middle of the wilderness. The home where she stayed was as basic as you could get, with a combined kitchen and living area on the first floor, and a ladder leading up to a loft that functioned as a bedroom. Minimal furniture, a power generator, and a well system for water, and she was set.

For how long she had no idea.

A large pond was situated within walking distance, about half a mile down a steep hill from the flat area on which the cabin was situated. The presence of water so close and nature all around her was what she'd been wishing for and dreaming of since the day she'd lost them. She'd felt incomplete, living only half a life. Now she had it, but pure happiness still lay out of reach.

She missed Castor. His absence was a hole inside her, an ache that no amount of time would fix.

Only three days had passed since she'd left. Disappearing on him had come with a certain amount of guilt, even if she was doing this to protect him. When you loved someone, sacrifice came with the gig. Right?

"Leia."

She could've sworn she heard his voice on the wind calling her name. Fabulous. Now she was hearing things. Not even the loss of her spring had made her lose her sanity.

"Leia, it's Castor. Honey, are you in there?"

She dropped the glass she was drying with a hand towel, hardly hearing the sound of it shattering in the sink.

No. He couldn't be here. This had to be a trick.

Cautiously, she moved to the window at the front of the cabin and inched back the edge of the white linen curtain to peer outside. Sure enough, Castor Dioskouri stood in the field of wildflowers outside her new home.

By the gods. Her eyes drank in the sight of casual jeans, a short-sleeved black T-shirt, and hiking boots. The wind ruffled up his dark hair. She gulped, battling the need to run outside and pitch herself into his arms even as she knew she had to throw him off the property. Now.

Leia took a deep breath before she pulled open the door. Hands on her hips, she confronted him. "What are you doing here?"

She glanced at the tall pine trees around them but caught no trace of the protection by which she was supposedly surrounded. Where had they been when a demigod walked right onto the property. Huh?

His intense, blue-eyed gaze zeroed in on her, and he stalked across the field toward her. "I'm here to be with the woman driving me absolutely crazy."

Her heart picked up its pace trying to punch through her ribs. She ignored it and tilted her chin. "I left you."

"I noticed." He stopped only a foot away.

The scents of clear blue sky and his spicy aftershave, her gift to him, floated across the distance to curl around her, making the ache of longing in her heart worse.

"You didn't give me two weeks' notice."

That's what this was about? "There's a letter in the top drawer of my desk. Delilah will help you with a smooth transition to a new executive assistant."

His lips pinched and he crossed his arms, a sure sign of major irritation. "Would she help me find another nymph?"

She glanced away, her jaw tight. Sex. He wanted the sex.

"One who has the ability to see straight into my soul? One who challenges me with her refusal to back down or let my ego take over? One whose kisses brought me out of a thousand-year sleep?"

She slowly turned her head, eyes wide…hope, doubt, and fear all warring for dominance inside her. "What are you saying?"

He stepped closer, crowding her. "I'm saying I don't want to lose you. Don't walk away."

Hope was winning the battle, but she couldn't let it. He loved his dead wife. "I'm a good assistant, but Delilah can find you another."

He took her by the shoulders and gave her a small shake. "I'm not talking about losing my assistant."

"I've only been something…more…to you for a few days."

He stole her move and rolled his eyes heavenward. "You've been more to me for months. Perhaps even a year."

Oh, gods. A trembling started up inside her. Was that true?

Her heart surged, but before she could respond or even gather her thoughts, a deep voice interrupted. "How sweet."

She and Castor both whipped toward the sound of Kaios's voice. The ancient werewolf stepped out of the cover of the dark woods.

Dammit. "*This* is what I was trying to keep you out of," she hissed at Castor.

"Trying to protect a demigod?" Kaios, whose keen ears had picked up her comment, pulled his lips back in a sneer of derision as he advanced toward them. "You always did have an overblown sense of your powers, nymph."

Behind him, out of the darkness, a line of wolf shifters, already in their animal form, advanced upon them. The fur bristled on their backs, ready to attack. There had to be at least twenty or more.

How and why had they followed Kaios? Where had they come from? Tala and Marrok would be pissed.

Kaios flicked a hand and a low growl rose from a few, while others pulled back their lips, baring their teeth in snarls meant to terrorize.

Castor stepped closer and took her hand, presenting a united front. Above them, the skies darkened with the warning of his wrath, swirling with dark clouds.

"Oh, I have a way to deal with you." Kaios turned to signal someone over his shoulder. A woman with deep red hair stepped out of her hiding spot. She raised her arms and whispered words Leia couldn't catch. The clouds cleared in an instant, returning to the blue skies of moments before.

Castor's hand twitched in hers.

"What's she doing?" she asked under her breath.

"Best guess is she's a witch."

The woman closed her eyes, her face a study of regret. Leia got the impression the woman would rather be anywhere than here right now. If the witch could control nature, could she keep Leia from using her own powers? Being located near a large body of water hadn't been coincidence. Closing her eyes so Kaios couldn't see them glow, she reached for her powers, and slammed into a mental wall. Her eyes flew open.

"I'm sorry," the woman mouthed at her, misery pinching her white face.

The woods hushed, going eerily quiet—no bird chirped, no animals scurried through the underbrush. They'd all gone into hiding. Were Leia's fellow nymphs equally disabled?

"Your brothers and sisters will be no use to you now, Lyleia."

There was her answer, but Leia wasn't worried. Yet.

"Why don't we make this fight a tad more even, first," Marrok's voice boomed from behind her. Together, he and Tala stepped out of the line of woods at her back, along with their own contingent of wolf shifters.

Kaios's smug smile fell. "You'd go against your own people? Against one of your ancestors? And risk bringing werewolves on your heads?"

"We'll kill you if we get the chance," Tala snarled.

At an unseen signal, both sides of wolves burst into a dead run, straight at each other. Before her eyes, both Tala and Marrok shifted, the action immediate, rending their clothes and accompanied by their twin yelps of agony as their bones realigned. In seconds, chaos reigned all around them.

Castor grabbed her and slung her onto his back. "Hold on tight."

Before she could say a word, he took off. The glen, then the forest, blurred around her as his phenomenal speed took them down to the pond. He deposited her at the edge of the water. The only reason she didn't protest was the fact that she'd needed to get to the pond anyway.

But now she couldn't keep Castor with her. She tugged on his hand. "You have to knock the witch unconscious."

He leaned down to plant a quick, hard kiss on her lips. "I know."

And he was gone.

"We can't use our powers."

Leia spun around to find Calliadne and ten other Naiad sisters standing hip-deep in the pool behind her. "There's a witch."

Calli scowled. "I swear the Covens Syndicate is asking for a war."

"I suspect this witch is being forced to cooperate with Kaios against her will."

"You always were a smart girl." Kaios stood at the edge of the trees, not ten feet from her. He must've guessed where Castor had taken her and followed.

Sounds of the violent battle above them echoed off the peaks of the mountains all around—snarls and growls, yelps of pain and howls of rage. She tried to sense the water, pull it under her control, but nothing happened. Castor had to find that witch. Soon.

She kicked off her flip-flops, her feet squelching into the mud as she stepped back. The water lapped at her ankles, then her knees, plastering her jeans to her legs. She waited for the buzz and flow of the water as it absorbed into her.

Nothing happened.

Kaios paced at the edge of the trees, not coming nearer the pond. "One night together. Was that too much to ask?"

The man was obsessed. "Way too much," she snapped.

He continued his pacing. "You shouldn't have attacked me in front of my people. People I intended to lead. It took me centuries to regain my status within the werewolf community."

"Killing me won't help. Even if you win today, you'll be hunted down. The entire community of nymphs and the Banes and Canis packs of wolf shifters—and all their allies—

are going to want your blood."

Not to mention Castor bringing down the wrath of the gods.

"I've been alive much longer than you, little girl. Feuds pass, anger fades. I'm still here."

The tips of her fingers tingled with an achingly familiar sensation.

Thank the gods. Castor must've been successful. Expression carefully neutral, she backed farther into the water, closer to her sisters. They had to time this right. They'd tried to drown him before and failed.

She hadn't meant for him to live all those years ago. Not with the way he kept coming at her.

Leia gathered her power inside her, secretly whispering her will to the water surrounding her, using it to whisper instructions to her sisters. They communicated better fully submerged, but even being up to her waist, as she was now, helped.

"Do you want to know why I rejected you?" She needed to distract him a bit longer.

Kaios aimed a bored expression her way. "No. I want you to die."

Without warning, he held up the gun she hadn't seen in his hand, pointed it at her, and pulled the trigger.

A wall of water surged up in front of her and turned to solid ice in an instant. The bullet lodged in the block. She dropped it into the pond with a splash. Before Kaios could react, she and her sisters worked together. They tossed a wave up over him, and tendrils of water lilies wrapped around his legs and arms.

Werewolves might be incredibly powerful, but nature in her fullness was a murdering bitch that nothing could stand against.

They dragged him, kicking and screaming, into the water,

pulling him to the center of the pond, where they forced him under. His screams turned into a gurgle of terror as his head submerged. They held him under for ten solid minutes until the thrashing slowed, his eyes rolled back in his head, and his struggles ceased. To be sure he was dead, they kept him under even longer, until the water reeked with the taint of death.

Leia closed her eyes, waiting for relief or perhaps a sense of justice served. But she was numb.

"What do you want us to do with him?" Calli asked.

"I don't care." Leia trudged back out of the water, inexplicably exhausted. Kaios's death, and her revenge, had been a long time coming. Most of the time, she'd doubted this moment would ever arrive. Now that it had, other than knowing he couldn't hurt anyone else, she just didn't care.

She flopped down at the edge of the pond, her clothes once more dry as a bone. The fight up by the cabin must've wound down, because the sounds of the battle no longer rang through the trees.

"What will you do?" Calli asked.

Leia considered the last thing Castor had been saying to her when Kaios appeared.

"I don't know."

"What about Castor?"

Leia ran a hand over her face. "Do you think there's a chance for a son of Zeus and a failed nymph?"

"I think love is worth trying for."

"I'm not worthy of his love."

Calli floated out of the water, her own diaphanous dress of white drifting in the breeze, also instantly dry. Her sister sat beside her and took her hand. "We weren't worthy of your love. I should have been there for you. We should have supported you all these years. We're family."

Leia blinked away unwanted tears. "I always understood."

"That doesn't make it right."

Calli wrapped her arms around Leia's shoulders. "You are worthy, sweetie. The question is, is he worthy of you?"

Chapter Seventeen

"Lyleia, can you come in here, please?" Castor's deep voice sounded on the intercom on her desk.

She frowned at the tone to his voice, one that didn't seem quite right. She couldn't put her finger on it, but he sounded almost...nervous. She didn't like it. What had those gods been saying to him?

After the fight with Kaios, Castor had taken them both home to Austin. While he had once again insisted on sitting beside her on the flight, he'd been surprisingly quiet during the trip, and he hadn't brought up their earlier conversation. For once, Leia had no clue what to say, so she hadn't said anything either. Back home, he'd driven her to her apartment.

He hadn't come in. "Do you trust me?" he asked.

"Yes."

"I need to arrange something. After that I'd like us to have a talk, but it might take me a day or two to wrap up this other thing. Will you wait—don't make any plans or run off again—until then?"

"We can't talk now?" Despite her long life, waiting now

would be awful.

He gazed at her with a strange urgency. "No. This other thing needs to happen first."

She'd frowned but agreed.

"Come into the office like normal tomorrow," he'd said.

Even weirder, but okay. He escorted her to her door, which had a fresh coat of paint and a gleaming new lock. She raised her eyebrows, and he shrugged. "I may have broken your door the day you left."

He'd been that desperate? She shook her head, holding back a smile. "You and that god complex of yours, Superman."

He chuckled, then leaned down and feathered a ghost of a kiss across her lips. "I'll see you tomorrow."

She'd watched, confused and lost, as he walked away, hands stuffed in his pockets, head bowed. Something was seriously wrong with Castor. Was he regretting those words to her in the glen? Their nights together? His kiss gave her a small amount of hope that regret wasn't his issue. But if it wasn't, what was?

Those questions had kept her up half the night. Her apartment, usually a place of comfort for her, had been more like a cage, and time her enemy as she waited for whatever came next.

Then this morning, she'd come into the office as requested, both eager to see him and dreading how he'd treat her. Castor was already there, the door closed between them. She resisted the temptation to barge in and demand what was up with him. He'd asked for her trust. So, curiosity and a need to be with him dragging at every action, she'd forced herself to get down to the usual routine, checking through a week's worth of emails from her absence.

Around nine a.m., two gods she'd recognize anywhere had shown up in her office—Zeus and Poseidon.

The hairs stood up on the back of her neck as pure power

pulsed through the room. Contrary to popular movies, they didn't wear long robes and sport gray beards. Nymphs had a hard time resisting gods for a reason, and the power they exuded, a strong aphrodisiac by itself, wasn't the only draw. Both appeared as young men, in their early thirties at most. Like their demigod offspring, both had broad shoulders, trim hips, and likely sported six-packs under those immaculate suits. Romanticized images of the perfect male body got the original blueprint from these immortals. Both were devastatingly handsome, though Zeus was dark—black hair, deep brown eyes—where Poseidon was fair—blond hair and green eyes.

They did nothing for her.

Leia sent Poseidon a hate-filled glare, then moved her gaze to Zeus, head held high. "May I help you?"

"We have an appointment with my son," Zeus said, his voice a rumbling roll of thunder.

So that's where Castor got his sexy, deep tones from.

"Come on in, Dad," Castor called from his office.

The gods gave her a polite nod before entering Castor's office, closing the door behind them. They'd been in there about an hour before Castor had called her in. Now, she smoothed the slim skirt of her deep red suit over her hips and checked the V of the jacket, which showed just enough cleavage. She'd forgone a blouse underneath this morning when she'd dressed, determined to remind Castor what he was missing. With a soft *click*, she opened the door and the three men all standing together in front of Castor's modern glass desk turned to face her.

Castor's expression gave nothing away. Damn, he looked amazing in her favorite black suit and maroon tie. With effort, she pulled her gaze away. Zeus appeared amused, if the quirk of his lips was anything to go by. Poseidon she refused to look at again. She might do something stupid like try to drown the god of the oceans with the water in the bottle on her desk.

That was until he crossed the room to stand before her, surrounding her in a cloud of salty sea air.

"Kaios caused a lot of problems for you."

She raised her eyebrows pointedly, and he held up his hands. "Granted, I was part of the situation. Now he's dead, I would like to make amends."

She crossed her arms. "Oh, really?"

His mouth tightened, but he didn't say anything about her rudeness. Gods didn't take sarcasm well most of the time. "Yes. His death negates my deal with him, an agreement bound by an unbreakable oath. Now I am no longer beholden by my word, and I can release your spring."

Her arms dropped to her side even as her mouth dropped open. "What do you mean by release it?"

"You assumed it buried and gone, but it's simply deep underground. I can raise it to the surface again."

"You're saying I can…" She swallowed. "I can go home?"

After ages without it, hope was no longer an emotion she attached to her life's purpose as a nymph.

She glanced at Castor but encountered a stony expression. He was keeping his thoughts close. She pulled her gaze back to the god standing before her.

"Yes. Would you like that?"

She was tempted to roll her eyes at the fatherly tone to his voice and patronizing expression on his face. He thought he was doing her a favor. After all this time? Gods. They never changed.

She considered his question. Would she like that? Up until a year ago, she had been desperate for her spring. But now…

Another glance at Castor told her nothing. *I guess that tells me everything.* She turned back to Poseidon, her gaze steady, which was more than she could say for her shaking hands. "Yes. I would like you to bring my spring back."

He inclined his head. "Consider it done." He paused

expectantly.

"If you're waiting for me to thank you, you'll be waiting centuries. That's how long it's taken you to put this right."

His eyebrows drew low over his eyes, but she tipped her chin and stared him down. Eventually, he turned to Zeus. "I'll wait for you by the elevators."

That's right, asshole. Run away. She glared after his departing back before turning to Zeus. "I assume I have you to thank for this?"

He crossed the room and took her hands in his. "I may have suggested my brother consider this action."

"Thank you."

"Don't thank me. Thank my son."

Her heart sank at the realization that Castor was trying to get rid of her. "I will."

Zeus studied her, those sharp eyes taking in every nuance of her appearance. "I can see the appeal."

Rather than worry she had yet another god on her tail, she could tell he meant it as an impartial observation. "Thank you."

"You've been good for Castor. I thank you."

She glanced between the two men with wide eyes. "All I've done is keep his business life organized."

He shook his head. "You've done much more."

"Father." A warning note deepened Castor's voice.

Leia didn't know what to say, so she said nothing.

Zeus tipped his head. "After my brother releases your spring, you still have a choice, you know."

"I know." She did. She'd lived without her spring this long; she was fully aware what her options were.

He searched her eyes. What he found there must've pleased him because he gave a satisfied nod. Then he drew her forward and kissed both her cheeks. "Castor is not made of steel, though he'd like you to believe he is," he murmured in her ear.

She wasn't entirely sure where he was going with that comment, but she also felt the truth behind the words. "I know that, too."

He gave her a warm smile. "I believe you do."

He turned and gave Castor a wave, receiving one in return. "Make good choices," he called over his shoulder as he sailed out of the room.

Leia swung around to gaze at Castor, who stared right back. She cleared her throat. "Thank you for that."

He shrugged. "It's the least I could do."

She didn't know what to do with her hands, so she clasped them in front of her. Why was he being distant?

She waved at the door. "I'll get back to work."

He moved around his desk, sat, and turned his attention to his computer, effectively dismissing her. "When should I expect your resignation?"

She paused at the doorway. She couldn't turn to face him, certain he'd see the devastation written on her face. He truly didn't want her. Granted, she shouldn't be surprised since they'd never discussed anything beyond a temporary attraction. However, after what he'd said in the glen before Kaios had appeared…apparently, she still had the capacity to hope in vain.

"I'll call Brimstone today and have my official letter to you before I leave."

She closed the door behind her with a *click*. On unsteady legs, she crossed the office to her desk. She sat, her gaze on her black computer screen, not really seeing it, too preoccupied trying to keep her tears at bay.

Who knew when she finally got her wish to return to her spring granted, she'd be reluctant to go?

After several minutes, when she felt more in control, she picked up the phone and dialed a familiar number. "Hello, Delilah…"

Chapter Eighteen

"Are you a total idiot? Or just blind as the Graeae when Perseus stole their eye?"

Castor checked his watch, noting the late hour. How had she known he was still at work? "Hello, Delilah."

"Leia is perfect for you. What the hell are you doing replacing her?"

"Poseidon is giving her spring back."

"I heard." No give in Delilah's voice.

"She's going home."

"Does she want to?"

He frowned. "Of course she wants to."

"She said that?"

He ran his hand through his hair and leaned back, his chair creaking a protest. "I heard her talking to Calliadne after the fight. They didn't know I was there, and she said she wasn't worthy of me. Because she thinks she's a failed nymph."

"So, you arranged to have that failure fixed…" Delilah guessed.

"Yes. And she chose the spring." Gods that hurt. His heart had been bleeding since. "I have to let her go."

"Why?"

Delilah wasn't usually this dense. "She's been lost without her spring for over a millennium."

"Until recently, I would've agreed with you."

He scowled, getting tired of the riddles. "What does that mean?"

"It means she's perfect for you."

"You said that already, and I agree. She's been a terrific executive assistant."

"I'm not talking about the job." The level of frustration in her voice was so unlike Delilah, who never flapped, that Castor paused.

Hope, that deceptive emotion, sprang to life inside him. "What *are* you talking about?"

"I've never seen her happier than she has been this last year working for you. Especially right after Tala and Marrok's mating."

"But Kaios…"

"Don't get me wrong. He had her worried, but she was also more alive than she has been in…"

"In?"

"At least as long as I've known her, which includes before she lost her spring."

Castor thought back over the last year. Delilah was right. Leia had changed. When she'd first started with him, she'd been serious and distrustful of him. Over the course of the year, the real Leia had emerged—smart, still mouthy, and strong. Lately, she'd let him in more and more. Right up until today.

He gripped the phone. "Did she *tell* you why she's been so happy?"

"I think that's something you should discuss with Leia

herself."

• • •

Wrapped up in pajamas and a fleece robe, her hair still wet from a long soak in the tub because she couldn't be bothered to dry it, Leia plunked down on her sofa and put her feet up on her coffee table. With a little salute, she lifted a glass of red wine, a Christmas gift from Castor she had just opened, and gave a silent tribute to Dionysus. She had to hand it to the pleasure god—wine was good stuff. The full-bodied liquid slid over her tongue and she savored the chocolate and cherry aftertaste.

Closing her eyes, she lay her head back against the comfy cushion of her overstuffed chair and tried to relax away her gods-awful day. Pun absolutely intended.

A loud knock at her door startled her, and she jerked her hand, sloshing a few drops of her wine on her cream-colored cushion. "Damn. Damn. Damn."

She hopped up and ran to the kitchen, where she wet a rag, then back to the couch where she dabbed at the stain.

Whoever was at the door knocked again. Only louder. She glared at the door and wished whoever it was on a long trip across the river Styx. "Just a second."

"It's me."

She paused mid-dab at the deep, unmistakable rumble of Castor's voice. What was he doing here? More importantly, she couldn't take another round with him tonight. She was too emotionally drained.

She slowly went back to working at the stain. "What do you need?" she called.

"Let me in, please."

She ground her teeth. Rag clenched in her fist, she hopped up and crossed to the door, which she unlocked and opened a crack. By Olympus, he looked good. Edible. She loved it when he rolled back his sleeves. "I'm not in the best mood right now. Can it wait?"

"No."

Stupid question anyway. This was Castor. Patience was not his gift.

"Does it have anything to do with my replacement? I talked to Delilah today, and she'll be at the office tomorrow to get things rolling."

"I'm not here to talk about your damn job."

She opened the door wider and put her hands on her hips. "There's no need to swear at me."

Rather than answer, Castor stepped inside, invading her space and forcing her to back up. He kicked the door closed and yanked her into his arms. His lips covered hers in a kiss that blasted her senses and chased her questions and exhaustion to the back of her mind.

When he encountered no resistance, Castor framed her face with his hands and the kiss gentled—both reverent and drugging at the same time. Her body came alive beneath his scorching touch. Eventually, reluctantly, he pulled back. His blue eyes were almost navy, eyes she could drown in.

"I can't let you go." The words seemed ripped from a dark place within him.

Hope surged, but experience taught her not to trust it. She gazed at him warily. "Why?"

He swallowed. "Because I'm in love with you. And I think you're in love with me."

His words stole the breath from her lungs as happiness and relief poured through her like a tidal wave.

He gave her a little shake. "Say something."

She gave him a broad grin. "Something."

"Not what I was going for." While his lips twitched at her teasing, a worry lingered in his gaze she'd never seen before.

She didn't like it.

She slipped her arms up through his and around his neck and gave him a sweet, lingering kiss. "You're right. I love you, too."

The shadow in her heart must've reflected in her expression, because he didn't celebrate. "But?"

She swallowed. "I thought you'd shut out love for good after your wife." There. She'd said it.

"Ah." He smoothed the hair back from her face and ran a tender finger down her cheek. "I thought I had, too. But I've never felt for anyone what I do for you. It borders on irrational. I've been waiting thousands of years to find a love like this."

Leia's heart swelled. She went up on tiptoe to place a light kiss on his lips, inhaling his now- familiar scent. "So have I," she whispered.

"Thank the gods." His arms tightened around her almost painfully, but she didn't protest. He leveled a strangely intense look on her. "Be my wife, my partner in this unending, extraordinary life?"

She blinked, both her emotions and her mind still catching up, not expecting either a declaration of love or a proposal, let alone in the same night.

Before she could answer, he rushed into speech. "Don't say no. We can relocate. I've already started searching for property close to your spring."

She shook her head. "I'll trade with a nymph closer to here. A spring in Greece is a real find these days, so it shouldn't be difficult."

The tense muscles of his shoulders relaxed slightly. He searched her gaze. "Are you sure?"

"Yes." Gods yes. "Wherever you are is home for me."

Air punched from him and he leaned his forehead against hers. "I don't deserve you."

Instead of tossing off a joke, she kissed him gently. "You won my love with every good part of you."

"It doesn't hurt that I'm pretty hot, either." He waggled his eyebrows, so different from the solemn, often irritated Castor she'd started working for a year ago.

She rolled her eyes. "Did you know…"

For once he waited for the end of that statement.

She flashed a mischievous smile. "…vanity is just not sexy at all."

"I'll show you sexy." He swung her off her feet, into his arms, and strode toward her bedroom.

Leia wrapped her arms around her neck, snuggling against him in a delicious way, because she was allowed now. Free with him because forever was just on the horizon. "How about we take a bath," she whispered in his ear, and felt his shiver against her body.

Castor stopped walking, the evidence of his reaction to her words surging against her hip and driving her own need higher. "Are you sure?" he asked.

She nibbled at his ear. "I want to find out what all the hype is about. With you. I've been waiting to share this with the man I love."

Castor swallowed. With a grin that made her laugh, he changed direction. "Your request is my command."

Epilogue

Delilah sat behind her large and elaborately carved mahogany desk—a gift from a grateful phoenix—and kicked off her sky-high stilettos, scrunching her toes into the deep-pile carpet to relieve her cramping feet. The shoes worked for the image she insisted on projecting to the world, but boy did they kill.

She reached for the mail her assistant, Naiobe, had left neatly stacked in its tray. She opened the first envelope and smiled when she discovered a wedding invitation from Leia and Castor. About time, too. With a flick, she flipped over the envelope, scrunching her nose at the "and Guest" beside her name. Not that she'd be attending the wedding. She had a strict *no weddings, matings, funerals, or ceremonies in general* rule. Over the years, she'd found they weren't particularly fun.

She hadn't attended Tala and Marrok's mating ceremony either, despite the fact she'd arranged that particular union—a brilliant move on her part, if she said so herself. Or she would say so if they could figure out what the fuck wasn't working in that relationship. They'd done a good job of hiding it from people—after all, their union wasn't wanted by many in both their packs, and with the sign from the gods being faked, they couldn't exactly let others see the growing gulf between them.

But Delilah could tell.

Why were relationships so damn hard? She'd practically handed the wolf pair the perfect situation on a silver platter. They'd better not screw it up. She'd give them six months before taking matters into her own hands.

Couldn't be having dissatisfied customers, now could she?

Acknowledgments

No matter what is going on in my life, I get to live out my dream surrounded and supported by the people I love—a blessing that I thank God for every single day. Writing and publishing a book doesn't happen without the support and help from a host of incredible people.

To my readers (especially my Awesome Nerds Facebook fan group!)... Thanks for going on this ride with me. Sharing my worlds with you is a huge part of the fun. Castor and Leia's story started out with the idea of picking random supernatural creatures and making them fall in love. And boy did I find out how fun that is. I hope you fell in love with my nymph and demigod and their story as much as I did. If you have a free sec, please think about leaving a review. Also, I love to connect with my readers, so I hope you'll drop a line and say "Howdy" on any of my social media!

To my editor, Heather Howland...this was a rough one when it was supposed to be easy. Thank goodness we practically share a brain. Thanks for hanging in there with me.

To my Entangled family...best team in the business!

To my agent, Evan Marshall...you're my rock!

To my author sisters and friends...you are the people I feel most me with, and you inspire me every single day.

To my support team of beta readers, critique partners, writing buddies, reviewers, RWA chapters, writer's guild, friends, and family (you know who you are)...thank you, thank you, thank you.

Finally, to my own partner in life and our awesome kids...I don't know how it's possible, but I love you more every day.

About the Author

Award-winning paranormal romance author Abigail Owen grew up consuming books and exploring the world through her writing. She loves to write witty, feisty heroines, sexy heroes who deserve them, and a cast of lovable characters to surround them (and maybe get their own stories). She currently resides in Austin, Texas, with her own personal hero, her husband, and their two children, who are growing up way too fast.

Discover more Amara titles...

MALFUNCTION
a *Dark Desires Origin* novel by Nina Croft

It's been five hundred years since we fled a dying Earth. Twenty-four ships, each carrying ten thousand humans—Chosen Ones—sleeping peacefully...until people start dying in cryo. Malfunction or murder? Sergeant Logan Farrell is determined to find the truth. Katia Mendoza, hot-shot homicide detective, has been woken from cryo to assist his investigation, and Logan finds himself falling for her. But he doesn't know Katia's secret... It's not only humans who fled the dying Earth.

RED AWAKENING
a *Red Zone* novel by Janet Elizabeth Henderson

The mission is simple: find a way into CommTECH's state-of-the-art compound, bug the lead bio-engineer before the company releases an implant that will kill millions, and get out. But ex-Army Ranger Mace Armstrong can't leave Keiko Sato, CommTECH's brilliant, beautiful, and stubborn press secretary, behind. She has no idea what secrets he and his team are harboring, or that she's calling to the animal that's been locked inside of him for a century.

COLDEST FIRE
a novel by Juliette Cross

Archangel Uriel is hell bent on revenge on the demon prince Vladek. And he'll need the help of the last person he can trust—the demon witch Nadya. Using the fight pit circuits in the demon underworld, Nadya helps Uriel combat his way to the arena at the castle in Russia. Only she isn't what she seems. As a matter of fact, she may hold the key to his redemption...and to his heart.

Made in United States
Troutdale, OR
06/17/2024